Who dunnit?

At the sound of smashing glass right behind her and the earsplitting alarm, Elizabeth spun around. It took her a few moments to focus on what the problem was. Her mouth dropped open as she realized that the display window of Precious Stones had been broken. A young woman with a baby carriage was standing there, frightened, her hand over her mouth. Nearby, the clown who had been handing out balloons was staring in shock at the store window.

"Maria, look!" Elizabeth cried, already moving forward. Maria was right next to her, her video camera dangling at her side.

"What happened?" Maria asked. Then the two girls were surrounded by people swarming over to the sound of the alarm.

Staring at the jewelry store window, Elizabeth saw that the expensive gold watches, rings, and necklaces of the display window were gone.

"It was a robbery!" she cried.

Bantam Books in the SWEET VALLEY TWINS AND FRIENDS series.
Ask your bookseller for the books you have missed.

SWEET VALLEY TWINS AND FRIENDS

Robbery at the Mall

Written by
Jamie Suzanne

Created by
FRANCINE PASCAL

BANTAM BOOKS
NEW YORK·TORONTO·LONDON·SYDNEY·AUCKLAND

To Heather Michelle Danielle Robb

RL 4, 008-012

ROBBERY AT THE MALL
A Bantam Book / August 1994

Sweet Valley High® and Sweet Valley Twins and Friends® are
registered trademarks of Francine Pascal

Conceived by Francine Pascal

Produced by Daniel Weiss Associates, Inc.
33 West 17th Street
New York, NY 10011

Cover art by James Mathewuse

ISBN: 0-553-48116-9

Published simultaneously in the United States and Canada

Bantam Books are published by Bantam Books, a division of Bantam
Doubleday Dell Publishing Group, Inc. Its trademark, consisting of the
words "Bantam Books" and the portrayal of a rooster, is Registered in
U.S. Patent and Trademark Office and in other countries. Marca
Registrada. Bantam Books, 1540 Broadway, New York, New York 10036.

PRINTED IN THE UNITED STATES OF AMERICA

OPM   0 9 8 7 6 5 4 3 2 1

One

◇

"Elizabeth, you're supposed to be helping me with my new camera," Maria Slater said. It was Friday afternoon, and Elizabeth had gone home with Maria after school.

"Hmm?" Elizabeth Wakefield looked up absently from her book. "I'm sorry, Maria. Did you say something?"

Maria marched across her room and firmly took the book out of Elizabeth's hands. She closed it with a snap and set it down on her bed.

"You came over to help me with my new video camera, remember?" Maria complained. "How am I supposed to learn to film action scenes if you're just sitting there like a lump?"

A smile created a dimple in Elizabeth's left cheek. "I'm sorry, Maria," she said. She stood up and brushed her long, light-blond hair back over her shoulder. "It's just that I finally got the latest

Amanda Howard mystery from the library. I was on the waiting list for five weeks! I couldn't resist taking a peek at the first page."

"You're addicted to those books," Maria said with a grin.

Elizabeth nodded ruefully. "I know. I can't help it."

"Well, I have another mystery for you," Maria said. She held up her video camera. "How does this dumb thing work?"

Laughing, Elizabeth came over to look at the camera. "This is really nice. Where did you get it?"

"My dad just bought himself a better one, so he let me have it." Maria impatiently pushed her thick, springy black hair out of her face. "But it has so many knobs and buttons. I can't even tell what I'm supposed to be looking through. And I have to be able to use it by tomorrow!"

Elizabeth turned the camera around and showed Maria the viewfinder. Maria held it up to her eye.

"I can't see anything! Are you sure this is where I'm supposed to look?"

Biting her lip to keep from laughing, Elizabeth took the camera back and pointed to the front lens. "This black thing here is called a lens cap," she said seriously. "It's traditional to remove it before you start filming."

"Oh. I knew that." Maria snapped off the lens cover, then looked through the viewfinder again. "Ah. That's better." Taking a step back, she carefully swept the camera around her room. Then she started to focus on Elizabeth.

"This is great!" she exclaimed. "I had no idea

that being *behind* the camera could be as much fun as being in front of it!"

"Are you thinking of giving up acting to become a famous filmmaker?" Elizabeth asked, only half teasing. Just a few years ago, Maria Slater had been one of the hottest child actresses in Hollywood. She had been in several movies and made tons of commercials. But then she had hit that awkward age, when she was a little too old to play the cute child parts and a little too young to play teen parts. So when her roles had started to get fewer and farther between, her parents decided to move the family to Sweet Valley so that Maria could go to regular schools and lead a normal life.

"I don't think I could ever give up acting completely, but it might be smart for me to have something to fall back on. Just in case I never make it big as an actress again."

"Is that why you're filming the Boosters tomorrow?"

"Uh-huh. I offered, and they agreed. I figured it would be good practice for me." Maria peered through the lens at Elizabeth, then started walking closer and closer to her.

"Like the Boosters would ever turn down a chance to be on camera," Elizabeth joked. "Hey, watch it!" She put up her hand before Maria bonked her in the nose with the zoom lens.

The Boosters were Sweet Valley Middle School's cheering squad, and Elizabeth's identical twin sister, Jessica, was a member. They were scheduled to give a special performance at the Valley Mall the next day to celebrate the opening of a brand-new food court. Jessica had been talking about it for days.

Maria smiled. "Sorry. It's hard to tell how far away you are with this thing. I hope I get the hang of it before tomorrow. It's my first break as a filmmaker, and I want to do a good job. I didn't realize how complicated it would be—I always thought they pretty much just pointed the camera and shot."

"It would be nice to open your video tomorrow with a slow pan around the mall, to show the new food court," Elizabeth suggested. "Then you could have a long shot of the Boosters in formation, starting their show. During the rest of the video you could focus on each Booster doing something special. Like when Winston puts Grace Oliver on his shoulders. Or when Jessica is at the top of the pyramid. Or when Lila does her high jump, going back to shots of the whole group in between."

Maria's brown eyes were shining. "That sounds great! Let me write it down." She took a pad and pencil off her desk and started to jot some notes. "See, I knew it was a good plan to ask a reporter for help. You know how to look at things with a special eye."

"I'm going to cover the event for the next edition of *The Sweet Valley Sixers*," she confirmed. "I'll profile each new restaurant, and then have a follow-up article on the Boosters' performance."

"That sounds like fun. Can I help you, uh, *profile* the restaurants? I mean, you're going to sample the food at each of them, right?" Maria's face crinkled in a grin.

"Actually, I was only going to write about them. But you're right—I really should do some, uh, research." Elizabeth's blue-green eyes twinkled. "So we'll just have to work our way through the entire food court, starting tomorrow."

"All right!" Maria said, giving Elizabeth a high five. "Now, let's practice some more with the camera. You stand over there, and I'll pan over to you." She held up the camera and looked through it.

"May I offer some advice?" Elizabeth asked.

Maria swung the camera down. "Sure. What is it?"

"One, you're looking through the wrong hole. Two, the camera is upside down." Elizabeth tried hard not to giggle.

Maria frowned and looked at the camera. "Oh. I knew that."

"Please pass the squash," Mrs. Wakefield asked Elizabeth that night at dinner. "Elizabeth? . . . Elizabeth!"

"Huh? What?" Elizabeth looked up.

Her father leaned over and took the book off her lap where she had been hiding it.

"Dinnertime is family time, sweetie," he said. "Not reading time."

Elizabeth looked down at her plate. "Sorry. But it's the new—"

"Amanda Howard mystery!" everyone in her family chorused.

Blushing, Elizabeth picked up her fork and knife and began to cut a piece of pork chop.

"Oh, geez," Elizabeth's fourteen-year-old brother, Steven, complained. "I guess this means she's going to start snooping around again, trying to sniff out some nonexistent mystery. 'Who took my gym socks?'" he said in a falsetto voice. "'What clues did they leave? Oh, here's the *scent* of the trail!'"

Across the table from her, Jessica started to laugh. Elizabeth glared at her sister.

Elizabeth was only four minutes older than Jessica. Each girl had long blond hair, blue-green eyes, and a dimple in her left cheek, and both were sixth graders at Sweet Valley Middle School. But that was where the similarities ended. While Elizabeth was a good student and enjoyed school, Jessica saw her classes merely as an opportunity to catch up on the latest gossip and show off her newest outfits.

Jessica loved being a member of the Unicorn Club, an exclusive group of girls who considered themselves the most popular and prettiest girls in school. Their official club color was purple, the color of royalty, and each member tried to wear something purple every day. Most of the Unicorn Club members were also in the Boosters.

Elizabeth preferred to have just a few really good friends, like Maria, and her best friend, Amy Sutton, and her sort-of boyfriend, Todd Wilkins. Privately, she thought the Unicorns were snobs.

"Very funny," Elizabeth muttered.

"Steven, leave Elizabeth alone," Mrs. Wakefield said. "And please pass the squash, Elizabeth."

"Oh, sorry." Elizabeth handed her mother the squash.

"But it's true, Mom," Jessica said, smirking. "You know what she's like when she's in the middle of an Amanda Howard mystery. One time I came in and found her looking at her hairbrush with a magnifying glass."

"Find any lice?" Steven said, taking a big sip of milk.

"Steven! Not at the dinner table," Mr. Wakefield warned him.

"You use gel, I don't. I was seeing if you'd been borrowing my brush," Elizabeth said defensively.

"Now there's a life-or-death issue," Steven murmured.

"Shut up!" Elizabeth snapped.

Mrs. Wakefield sighed and put down her fork. "Can we please change the subject before people start getting sent to their rooms?"

"Yes," Jessica said decisively. "Let's talk about the big show tomorrow. You know, the Boosters all got special T-shirts to wear. It's one of our biggest public performances yet. Lila, Janet, and I have been working out new routines for two weeks." Lila Fowler was Jessica's best friend, when they weren't being best enemies, and Janet Howell was the eighth-grade president of the Unicorns and the Booster squad leader.

"That's terrific, Jess," her father said. "Are you nervous?"

"Nah." Jessica shook her head. "We've been rehearsing like crazy. I have my pyramid jump down cold. And Maria Slater is going to videotape the whole performance. We're hoping to use her tape as an audition to help us get other jobs. This could be the start of something really big for us." She looked around the table excitedly.

Elizabeth ate her salad silently, remembering Maria's difficulty with the camera that afternoon. *I just hope Maria remembers where the "on" button is,* she thought.

Two

◇

"Jessica! Wait until I've parked the van," Mr. Wakefield exclaimed the next morning. The Wakefield family had just arrived at the Valley Mall, and Jessica had tried to jump out of the van while it was still rolling.

"OK, but hurry up, will you? I've got to meet all the other Boosters for warm-ups." Jessica sat back in her seat, an anxious expression on her face. Then she turned to Elizabeth. "Where are you and Maria going to set up?"

"I don't know yet," her sister replied. "We'll have to look around for the best spot."

"Well, make sure Maria has a perfect view of the Boosters," Jessica said, flipping her hair back. "After all, we're trying two new routines today. It's important that she capture it all on film."

Next to Elizabeth, Steven rolled his eyes.

"I'll do my best," Elizabeth promised, hiding her grin.

"And if you need any exclusive Booster interviews for the *Sixers*, I can set them up."

"Thanks. I'll let you know."

The Wakefields' van stopped in a parking space, and Jessica shot out of her door. "See you guys later!" she yelled over her shoulder.

Once inside the mall, Steven soon ran into some of his friends, and they took off. Elizabeth spotted Maria by the center fountain, and told her parents good-bye.

"Hey, Elizabeth," Maria greeted her. "I'm glad you came early. Could you please check my camera one more time?"

"Sure." Elizabeth took Maria's camera and looked it over. "Lens cap off, check. Zoom lens on, check. Camera right side up, check."

"Ha ha." Maria took the camera back, held it up to her eye, and practiced sweeping it around the mall.

"Have you seen the new food court yet?" Elizabeth asked.

"How could I, with all this stuff going on?" Maria lowered her camera and gestured with her hand. The Valley Mall had gone all out to make the new food-court opening a major media event. There were clowns handing out free balloons, booths set up where you could have your picture taken with a cutout of someone famous, free food samples at each new restaurant, maps of the mall being given away—it made Elizabeth wonder where she should start first for her *Sixers* article.

"I better write down the names of all the new food places," she decided, taking out her pad. She wrote, "Restaurants: Taco Shack, Mexican food; Ding How's, Chinese; Spuds 'n' Stuffin', potatoes; Figaro's Pizza, pizza; Smootharama, fruit smoothies and frozen yogurt; Chicken Lickin', fried chicken; and the Dog House, hot dogs."

She looked up at Maria. "Wow. This is amazing."

Maria nodded. "I can't wait to try some of these places. It'll be fun reviewing them for the *Sixers*."

"Maybe we should ask Amy to help us—" Elizabeth looked up to see the Boosters forming a line. "Oops, we better get ready. The Boosters are about to start."

"Quick! Help me with my stuff," Maria asked. She slung her camera bag over one shoulder, and Elizabeth grabbed a smaller bag of supplies. They moved in front of the Precious Stones jewelry store, where Maria would have the best shot of the Boosters.

Bracing her feet, Maria held the camera up and started to focus on where the Boosters were standing in the middle of the food court. As Jessica had said, they were all wearing matching T-shirts that proclaimed: *The Valley Mall: An International Dining Extravaganza.* Under that they were wearing their usual bluish-purple pleated Booster skirt, white socks, and white sneakers.

"Miss! What are you doing?"

Elizabeth and Maria turned around to see a burly middle-aged security guard frowning at them.

"I'm taping the Boosters' performance," Maria explained.

"Well, you're too close to the store. You're blocking traffic. Move over." The guard gestured curtly with his nightstick for them to move into the open space of the mall.

Elizabeth frowned. She didn't see how they were too close. After all, there was a clown handing out balloons who was even closer than they were. But Maria shuffled her bag over with her foot, and Elizabeth followed her. They moved about ten feet away and a little to the left of Precious Stones. Maria held up her camera again as the Boosters fell into formation.

"What a grump," she muttered under her breath.

Elizabeth nodded and started to take notes for her article. "The excitement grew as Sweet Valley Middle School's Booster squad prepared to begin their routine. . . ."

"Will you move over!" Jessica hissed at Lila, trying to keep a big Booster smile on her face.

"*I'm* in place. *You* move over," Lila snapped back. She was standing in a row with the other front-line Boosters. Each of the girls, and Winston Egbert, the only male Booster, had her feet apart and her hands on her hips as the group faced the crowd.

Jessica shuffled over a few feet. *It's not fair,* she thought angrily. Lila was standing right in a little square of light streaming through a skylight in the roof of the food court. That's where Jessica wanted to be. After all her hard work, she deserved to be in the little square of light, not Lila. She took an experimental hop in the air, pretending to be warming up, but really she just wanted to see the cute way her skirt kicked up when she moved.

In her mind, she ran through their routine again: a couple of their regular cheers, then into the special acts they had created just for the food-court opening. They were going to end with their trademark Booster pyramid, where Jessica took a running leap and sprang to the top of a six-person structure.

When all the Boosters were in place, Jessica saw Janet Howell nod. Jessica put on a big smile, ignored Lila, and threw her arms out to her sides as the music started.

A little thrill of anticipation ran through Maria when someone hit the sound system. Loud, bouncy music flooded the area. She flipped the video camera up to her eye and pressed the "on" button firmly.

"One, two, three, go!" Janet cried, and the Boosters started moving in perfect synchronization. They leapt first one way, then the next, jumping high, sweeping low to the ground. Winston led them in cheers as the Boosters moved in complicated swirls and patterns.

For a split second, Maria looked over at Elizabeth. She was watching the Boosters and simultaneously scribbling notes as fast as she could in her notepad.

Maria concentrated on the Boosters again, zooming in on different members as they performed. This was a snap. What had she been worried about? She felt as natural and as in control behind the lens as in front of it.

Maria couldn't wait to see the finished videotape. It would be useful for Elizabeth's article, too—it would probably contain details that she otherwise would have missed. *Maybe I should even consider a career in photojournalism*, Maria mused. *Me and my video camera traveling around the world . . .* She focused the camera again to take in a shot of all the Boosters. Focusing was tricky, but she was pretty sure she'd gotten the hang of it.

"Give me a V!" the Boosters yelled. "Give me an A! Give me an L!"

The crowd yelled the letters back until they had spelled "Valley Mall." Then came the moment they had all been waiting for. The music started to build, and the crowd was tense with excitement.

The Boosters started their special, brand-new cheer:

> "Tacos, pizza, chicken!
> "Eggrolls, hot dogs, spuds!
> "Smoothies are so finger-lickin',
> "Come on and bring your buds!
> "To the Valley Mall! Valley Mall! Valley Mall food court!
> "An in-ter-na-tional dining extravaganza!"

Elizabeth turned to Maria. "Do they mean taste buds, or buddies?"

Maria looked away from her camera for a minute. "You got me."

" 'Come on and bring your buds.' That is so

stupid," came a sneering voice in back of them.

Elizabeth turned around to see Veronica Brooks standing with Caroline Pearce. She frowned. Veronica was one of the few people Elizabeth didn't like, and she doubted that she ever would. Not all that long ago, Veronica had done her best to break up Elizabeth and Todd—and she had almost succeeded. Then she had tried to frame Jessica for a series of thefts at Sweet Valley Middle School. Elizabeth had come up with a brilliant plan to expose Veronica, and Veronica had never forgiven her.

"It's just a cheer," Elizabeth said, defending the Boosters.

"Well, I guess you can't expect much from them. They're just amateurs, after all," Veronica said snidely. Then she and Caroline walked away through the crowd, giggling.

"Forget about her—she's a jerk," Maria said from behind her camera.

Elizabeth tried, but it wasn't easy. Veronica was so obnoxious. She turned her attention back to the performance.

Now came the Booster pyramid finale. Janet Howell, Amy Sutton, and Kimberly Haver were all on the bottom, on their hands and knees. They squinched up next to each other to make a strong base. Grace Oliver and Ellen Riteman were on top of them, making the second layer. Tamara Chase and Winston stood to the sides, leading them in cheers.

Jessica walked back about ten feet, concentrating. Then she ran toward the pyramid, her arms pumping at her sides. Winston stepped forward to spot her as she leapt up to the top. She gauged the distance, bounced, and—

Suddenly there was the crashing sound of breaking glass, followed immediately by a piercing alarm. The Boosters, startled, all turned around to see what had happened.

"Ohhh!" Ellen cried, as Janet started to wobble beneath her. Within a split second, the two layers of the pyramid had collapsed to the floor in a heap.

"Aiiieee!" Jessica screamed as she found herself flying through empty air. She bounced against Winston's shoulder and knocked him down, then tumbled to the floor herself.

At the sound of smashing glass right behind her and the earsplitting alarm, Elizabeth spun around. It took her a few moments to focus on what the problem was. Her mouth dropped open as she realized that the display window of Precious Stones had been broken. A young woman with a baby carriage was standing there, frightened, her hand over her mouth. Nearby, the clown who had been handing out balloons was staring in shock at the store window.

"Maria, look!" Elizabeth cried, already moving forward. Maria was right next to her, her camera dangling at her side.

"What happened?" Maria asked. Then the two girls were surrounded by people swarming over to the sound of the alarm.

Staring at the jewelry store window, Elizabeth saw that the expensive gold watches, rings, and necklaces of the display window were gone.

"It was a robbery!" she cried.

The gruff security guard was there, pushing past people roughly. "OK, OK," he was saying. "Break it up. Everyone clear out, move out of the way."

Elizabeth grabbed her pad and started making notes. "Eleven thirty-seven. Sound of breaking glass. Alarm." She looked around for suspects. If there had been anyone lurking about, she realized, they had long ago been swallowed up by the curious and startled crowd.

Now the security guard had pretty much cleared the area, and three police officers ran up. One of the policewomen stood in front of the store, looking around. "Seal all exits," she said into her walkie-talkie. "We have a probable felon in the area. Send for backup."

Eyes wide, Elizabeth wrote that down in her notepad. "Did you see anything?" she asked Maria.

"I don't think so." Maria shook her head. "I was too busy filming the Boosters. I swung around when I heard the glass, but all I saw was the broken window."

Just then Jessica limped up. "What's going on? Do you know that I fell from the top of the pyramid? I could have killed myself," she complained.

"There was a robbery," Elizabeth told her, pointing to the broken window.

Jessica's eyes went wide. "A robbery? Here in the mall? Right now? That's incredible."

The police started shooing people away. Elizabeth heard them asking if anyone had seen anything.

"I mean, what kind of lamebrain thief would rob

a jewelry store right in the middle of a Boosters performance? We hadn't even finished the pyramid yet." Shaking her head, Jessica limped back to where the other Boosters were talking in a tight circle.

Elizabeth and Maria just looked at each other.

Another policewoman came over to Elizabeth and Maria. "You two were standing right here when the alarm went off, weren't you?"

They nodded. "But I didn't see anything," Elizabeth explained. "I was watching the Boosters."

"Did you turn around when the alarm went off?" the policewoman asked.

Maria nodded again. "We both did. But I didn't see anyone who looked like a thief—no one was running away or anything."

"OK, thank you. Please call this number if either of you remember anything," the policewoman said. She gave Elizabeth a small card with the precinct's number on it.

"We will," Elizabeth agreed.

"Wow, a real robbery, right here in the mall," Maria said.

"Right under our noses," Elizabeth said slowly. Her mind started to whir. "Five minutes ago, a robbery took place in broad daylight, right under our noses—in back of hundreds of people who came to the food-court opening." She looked at Maria, disbelief written on her face. "*And no one saw a thing.*"

"What do you think it means?" Maria whispered.

"I don't know. But I'm going to find out."

Three

"Finally!" Elizabeth muttered. It was six-thirty on Sunday morning. Elizabeth had been peering out the front window for nearly half an hour, waiting for the morning paper to be delivered. At last she had seen Ricky Hammaker riding his bicycle up their street, his newspaper bag over his shoulder.

Elizabeth flung open the front door and stepped out on the walkway just as Ricky was letting the paper fly.

"Ouch! Thanks a lot, Ricky!" Elizabeth yelled, rubbing the side of her head.

"Oh, sorry, Jessica!" Ricky called over his shoulder as he rode away. "I didn't see you!"

Elizabeth didn't bother to correct him. Might as well let him think Jessica was the only one dumb enough to get hit in the head by the newspaper.

Once inside, Elizabeth ran down the hallway, then eagerly spread open the first section on the kitchen table looking for an account of the mall robbery of the day before.

"Ah!" Her eyes caught the headline: "Robbery at Valley Mall Has Local Police Stumped."

An hour later, Elizabeth was reading her own notes about the theft. The newspaper hadn't had much information.

"Goodness, Elizabeth," her mother said, coming into the kitchen. "You're up early for a Sunday."

"I'm working on this case," Elizabeth said without thinking. Then she jerked her head up. "Uh, I mean, I wanted to set my *place*. At the table. You know." But it was too late. Mrs. Wakefield's eyes had already narrowed.

"Elizabeth Wakefield, you're not thinking of poking your nose into this robbery, are you?"

Elizabeth's brain was whirring, trying to think up a reply that wouldn't be an outright lie.

"I certainly hope not," said Mrs. Wakefield. "After what happened with that whole charm-school episode . . ."

"But Mom, I was right in the end, wasn't I?" Elizabeth argued.

Not long before, Elizabeth had suspected that the couple running Sweet Valley's new charm school were phonies and up to no good. It turned out she was right, and she'd foiled the crooks as they were trying to rob the Wakefields' own house. But she had to admit her solving of the mystery hadn't been very smooth.

"That's beside the point," Mrs. Wakefield argued. "You took unnecessary risks, jumped to conclusions, and caused a lot of people embarrassment. Not to mention making a general pest of yourself." Mrs. Wakefield smiled wryly and came over to kiss Elizabeth's head. "Honey, you're very smart, and your mind loves solving mysteries and puzzles. But I want you to stick to your Amanda Howard books, and not get involved in real-life situations that could be dangerous."

Elizabeth sat glumly at the kitchen table. Part of her knew that her mom was right. After all, with the charm-school mystery Elizabeth had gotten herself, Maria, and Amy into major trouble before they had solved it.

"But Mom, I was right there at the mall—" she began.

"Honey," Mrs. Wakefield said firmly, "leave this to the police. I'm sure they can handle it." She turned around and began to assemble the ingredients to make pancakes.

"The paper says the police don't have anything yet. Hundreds of people were there, but the police can't find any clues or witnesses," Elizabeth said stubbornly.

"Elizabeth," her mother said in a warning tone.

"I'm going upstairs to get dressed," Elizabeth grumbled. She took her notepad and the first section of the newspaper and stomped upstairs.

How could her mom expect her to ignore a robbery that happened practically right in front of her eyes?

"Good morning, Jessica," Mrs. Wakefield said brightly as Jessica came into the kitchen.

"Hmph," Jessica said as she headed to the fridge to get some juice.

"Do you want bacon with your pancakes?"

"Yeah, I guess," Jessica muttered, plopping down in her seat at the table.

Mrs. Wakefield turned around, an exasperated look on her face. "How about a 'Yes, please'? What's the matter with *you* this morning? Between you and Elizabeth, I feel like we're in the middle of a rainy day."

"Maybe she looked in the mirror this morning," Steven said breezily as he slid into his seat and grabbed the sports section of the paper.

Jessica stuck her tongue out at Steven just as their father walked into the room.

Mr. Wakefield looked at her, then at his watch. "Isn't eight o'clock a little early to be sticking your tongue out?"

Mrs. Wakefield turned around from where she was mixing up batter. "Both Jessica and Elizabeth are in bad moods," she informed him. "I'm not sure why. Steven is, as usual, picking on whichever sister is around." She looked as though she was about to be in a bad mood herself.

"Well, in that case, there's only one thing to do," Mr. Wakefield said. "Grab your purse, Alice. We'll go out for a nice breakfast, just the two of us."

Mrs. Wakefield smiled at him and put the bowl of batter down with a thump. "What a lovely idea," she said. "I'll just be a minute." She practically flew out of the kitchen and upstairs.

Steven gazed at his father with an open mouth. "No fair," he said. "What about us?"

"If you were better company this morning, I'd be glad to have you join us," Mr. Wakefield said. "As it is, I guess you guys are going to have to make your own pancakes this morning."

Steven and Jessica stared at each other in outrage.

"It's all your fault!" Jessica hissed as soon as Mr. Wakefield had strolled out of the room.

"Is not!"

"Is too!"

"What's going on?" Elizabeth asked, coming back into the kitchen. "Where are Mom and Dad going?"

"Out to breakfast without us," Jessica snapped. "They think we're no fun to be around this morning. Can you believe that?" She glared at the bowl of lumpy batter on the counter.

"'Bye, kids!" their mother called from the front door.

"See you later," their father added cheerfully.

The front door slammed shut.

Elizabeth sighed. "Jessica, you start stirring the pancake batter. Try to get the lumps out. Steven, you set the table and pour us all juice. I'll put the bacon in the microwave."

"Hello?" Steven had reached the phone first. "Who? Elizabeth Wakefield? Yeah, I guess so, Officer. But why do you want to talk to her?"

Elizabeth jumped up from her chair and ran over to the kitchen phone. "Let me have it," she whispered. Why were the police calling her? It had to have something to do with the mall robbery!

"I don't know. Who told you she was observant?" Steven said annoyingly, keeping the phone out of Elizabeth's reach. "Are you sure you mean Elizabeth *Wakefield*?"

Elizabeth finally snatched the phone out of Steven's hands. He stepped away, laughing.

"Hello?" she said eagerly into the phone.

"Elizabeth?" Amy asked. "What is Steven's problem?"

Elizabeth turned to glare at Steven, who was still giggling. "He's a loser, he can't help it. What's up?"

"I was just wondering if you wanted to go for a bike ride. We could work off all those tacos we ate yesterday at the mall." After the excitement had died down, Elizabeth, Amy, and Maria had begun their survey of the new food-court shops.

"Yeah. It'll do me good to get out of this nuthouse," Elizabeth agreed. They decided where to meet and hung up.

"Steven?" she said as she headed out of the kitchen.

"Yeah?"

"Get a life."

"Jessica Wakefield, this means war!" Lila Fowler shouted across the booth at Casey's ice cream shop later that afternoon.

Jessica opened her eyes wide. "Lila, all I'm saying is, some of the Boosters sort of lost their concentration yesterday. Ordinarily it wouldn't matter, but it was during our most important show ever."

Tamara looked confused. "We all heard a huge crash and then an earsplitting alarm. Of course we lost our concentration."

"A Booster should never lose her concentration during the pyramid," Jessica said firmly. "After all, I could have killed myself."

"Oh, please!" Lila looked disbelieving. "You're exaggerating. And no one was even looking at our stupid pyramid when the Valley Mall's biggest robbery was taking place right in front of us!"

"Not looking at our pyramid?" Jessica stared at Lila. "Lila, for your information, the famous Wakefield pyramid is the Boosters' trademark."

"*Wakefield* pyramid?" Janet demanded. "Since when is it the Wakefield pyramid? It's the *Booster* pyramid!"

Jessica sensed that she had gone too far. "Look, guys. Fine, it's the Booster pyramid. I'm only trying to suggest that a good Booster—"

"Good Booster!" Lila shrieked. People in Casey's turned around to look at their table. Lila lowered her voice. "Jessica Wakefield, are you saying that I'm not a good Booster?"

"I'm not saying that at all," Jessica said. She shrugged and took another sip of her strawberry milk shake. "Some Boosters are just better than others. That's all I'm saying."

"Fine!" Lila smacked her spoon down on the table. "The contest begins now. We'll find out who's a better Booster—you or me."

Jessica looked startled. "Contest?"

"What's wrong—are you chicken?" Lila taunted her.

"No way. But why bother with a contest? You know I'll win." Jessica was angry now.

"We'll find out, won't we?" Lila said with a sly smile.

"Yeah! And what do I get when I win?" Jessica demanded.

Lila thought for a moment, frowning.

"I have an idea," Janet said. "You know how we're supposed to dress up in fancy costumes to promote the food court at the black-tie party next Saturday night?"

"Yeah, so?" Jessica asked.

"Mrs. Richter, the lady who hired us, says we'll each wear a different costume at the party to represent the different restaurants. Well, whoever wins this contest, Jessica or Lila, gets to have first pick of costume, and the loser takes the last one." Janet paused importantly. "And the rest of us get to decide what the contest should be."

Jessica looked doubtful. "Just a costume? That doesn't seem like much of a prize."

Lila's eyes narrowed. "It's good enough for me. I'll be happy to win just to show Jessica who's the better Booster."

"Fine," Jessica snapped. "May the best Booster win!"

"Elizabeth, I thought we were going to the park," Amy called.

Elizabeth looked up and turned quickly to the left. "Sorry," she panted, pedaling hard to catch up with Amy. "Let's stop under the big oak tree. I have to talk to you."

Five minutes later the girls had dropped their bikes on the grass by their favorite tree. Elizabeth fished around in her backpack and pulled out her notepad.

"What's that?" Amy asked.

"Preliminary notes on the mall robbery," Elizabeth replied.

Amy's eyes widened. "Uh-oh."

Elizabeth frowned. "What do you mean, 'uh-oh'?"

"It's just that last time—"

"Do you want to hear these notes or not?" Elizabeth cut in.

"Sure I do," Amy said quickly.

Elizabeth rustled through her notepad pages. "OK. Now, the paper this morning said basically what we already know. In the middle of the Boosters' performance, everyone heard breaking glass and an alarm going off. No one saw anything."

Elizabeth consulted her notes again. "I wrote down my impressions of the moments after it happened, but it's only two lines: *No one running away. Why didn't security guard see anything?* I also wrote down the time it happened, and what the policewoman said." She read that, too.

"Hmmm." Amy looked thoughtful.

"This morning I asked Jessica and Steven what they had seen. I'll read it to you. Jessica: 'I was concentrating on our routine. Too bad the other Boosters weren't doing the same. All I noticed was people smiling at me, clapping along with my cheers. The next thing I saw was the pyramid crumbling, and then I fell and landed on the floor. My knee hurt, and I—'" Elizabeth smiled apologetically. "She didn't really have anything useful to add."

Amy snickered behind her hand. "Good old

Jessica. The Boosters did look great yesterday—until we fell, that is. How did Maria's movie come out, by the way?"

Elizabeth's face brightened. "I don't know yet. Are you going to Lila's house tonight to watch it?"

"Of course—I'm a Booster. I can't wait to see it. Our first major public performance."

"It should be great," Elizabeth agreed. "Now, let me read what Steven said. 'Well, Cathy and I weren't really watching the show too much. I mean, I hadn't seen her in a few days, and we were sort of sitting on that bench by the fountain. The one behind the big palm. She was filling me in on a math assignment I had missed—'" Elizabeth sighed and quit reading.

"Which means Steven and Cathy Connors didn't see anything because they were making out behind a big plant," Amy concluded.

"Right. No help there. I can't help feeing like I'm missing something," Elizabeth mused. "Something important—right in front of my face."

"What would Christine Davenport do right now?" Amy asked, only half teasing. Christine Davenport was always the heroine in Amanda Howard's mysteries.

"Hmmm. I think she would try to gather clues. And maybe interview possible suspects. She'd also have a map of the area, to see where anyone could have hidden, or found an escape route. After all, the police sealed the exits yesterday, but they didn't catch anyone trying to leave. That must mean something."

"Yeah," Amy agreed. "But what?"

Four

"Hi! Come on in," Lila said cheerfully when Elizabeth and Jessica arrived at her house that evening.

"Hi, Lila," Elizabeth said. "Ready to watch Maria's video?"

"Yep. The VCR's fired up," Lila replied, showing them into the large family room. Lila's parents had divorced when she was very small, and she and her father lived by themselves in one of the most opulent houses in Sweet Valley. Elizabeth thought Mr. Fowler spoiled Lila because he had to be away on business so much.

"How's that ankle, Jess?" Lila asked innocently.

"Fine," Jessica said between clenched teeth.

Elizabeth smiled to herself. All during dinner, Jessica had been complaining loudly about her twisted ankle. According to her, Lila had somehow sabotaged her during the high-jump contest—the first event to prove who was the best

Booster. The score so far was Lila, one; Jessica, zip.

"Make yourselves at home," Lila said, waving them toward one of the big leather couches. "Popcorn is over there, sodas are by the wet bar."

The doorbell rang again, and Lila left them to answer it.

Jessica and Elizabeth said hello to the rest of the Boosters—Johanna Porter and Melissa McCormick.

Maria and Amy followed Lila into the room a minute later, and the group was complete.

"Here it is," Maria said proudly, waving a video-cassette case in the air.

"Have you watched it yet?" Janet asked eagerly.

"No. I wanted to save it so we can all watch it together," Maria explained. "But I'm sure it came out OK. I can feel it." She paused, trying to explain. "I can just tell. It's like how I felt when I knew I had done a scene really well." She shrugged. "I might have to abandon acting altogether if my filmmaking career really takes off."

"OK, how about less talk and more movie?" Tamara said impatiently. She took a big handful of popcorn and passed the bowl to Grace Oliver, who was sitting next to her.

"Fine, are we all here?" Lila looked around the room. Then she turned to Maria, who was holding the remote. "Roll it!"

Winston Egbert jumped up and flicked off the lights.

Everyone settled back.

Feeling a thrill of anticipation, Maria clicked the

remote from where she was sitting. This was it—her big moment. She felt the way she used to when she, her parents, and her sister Nina attended one of her Hollywood premieres. She hadn't even seen it yet, but she was so proud of her movie. Long shots, pans, close-ups—she had used them all.

The large-screen TV made scratchy static sounds, then everyone squealed as the picture on the screen burst into life.

Maria held her breath as the colorful screen was suddenly replaced by a large pink blob. As the blob receded, it became Maria's thumb. Then the camera swung around, and they saw an out-of-focus close-up of the left side of Elizabeth's face. In the background were hazy views of bustling mall activity—people walking by, clowns handing out balloons, and in a tiny corner of the screen, a clump of Booster-like blobs huddled in a circle.

Maria frowned. "This is where I was getting set up. The real movie will start in a minute."

Onscreen, Elizabeth's fuzzy face leered toward the camera. "No, point the camera toward the Boosters," her voice said.

Around her in Lila's family room, Boosters giggled, and Maria smiled. Touches of humor were important in every movie. This showed that although she was a serious filmmaker, she still knew how to reach out and touch people's sense of fun.

"Pass the popcorn, please," Melissa said.

Then everyone erupted into cheers and whistles as the camera focused on the Boosters in the center of the food court. They were lining up, getting ready to start their first cheer. The picture snapped sharply into focus, then gradually drifted out to be just a little fuzzy.

"Focus!" a couple of people shouted.

"How come I'm cut off at the other end?" Grace complained.

"Just a minute," Maria muttered, feeling confused. The image on the screen wasn't at all like what she had remembered filming the day before. She was starting to wish that she had watched the video at home first. Then she could have edited out these first few awkward moments.

The picture on Lila's big-screen TV wobbled dizzily, then the Boosters were replaced by a lengthy view of one of Elizabeth's sneakers. It was scuffed and dirty, and Elizabeth's pinkie toe was poking out through a small hole.

"How fascinating," Janet said dryly. "Maria, did you get any shots of the Boosters at all?"

Maria's face was starting to feel warm. Had she brought the wrong video? Had her sister switched them at home? But no—the Boosters once again appeared on the screen, and their bouncy music came through loud and clear on the tape. There was a shot of Tamara doing some high kicks, but the image was so far away that she looked like a Munchkin. Then other Boosters crowded in next to Grace as they did a group cheer, but they looked weird and distorted, as though they had been filmed through a fish-eye lens. Suddenly the image zoomed so that Janet's face completely filled the screen of the TV—about three feet wide. It was so close that the pores of her skin were visible. So was a tiny pimple developing on her chin.

"Maria! What were you doing?" Janet shrieked.

"Nothing," Maria said quietly. She just didn't understand what had happened. Had Elizabeth told her the wrong things to do?

Maria's stomach clenched as the camera swung nauseatingly to one side, leaving the Boosters in the back of the frame, very small and very out of focus. A huge pink thumb lurched toward the camera so fast that several members of the audience involuntarily drew back away from the TV. By now Maria was swallowing hard, trying to get down the lump in her throat.

The image turned upside down, and for the next minute and a half the only thing they could see was a perfectly focused, extreme close-up of Maria's nostrils, filling the TV screen.

"Cool," Winston said, munching on popcorn. "It looks like a train's about to come out."

Maria felt hot tears start to well up in her eyes.

The black tunnels of Maria's nose gave way to another perfectly focused close-up of Elizabeth's right eye, staring fixedly into the camera. It blinked once. In the background the Boosters' music was blasting away, and they could hear people clapping along. The special food-court cheer began.

Elizabeth's eye looked away, blinked again, and then her disembodied voice asked, "Are you sure you're looking through the right hole?"

In Lila's family room, everyone except Maria and Elizabeth shouted, "No!"

For a split second Maria was glad to see the screen fill with Boosters, smiling and cheering and jumping up high. The camera panned perfectly from left to right down the line of cheerleaders: Janet, Tamara, Ellen, Lila, Winston, Grace, Amy, Kimberly, and Jessica. They looked great—totally in sync and enthusiastic.

Everyone watching the TV cheered and clapped. "Go, Boosters!" Kimberly said, punching the air.

"Finally!" Jessica said.

Then there was another wild, dizzy sweep off the Boosters and over to a white column in the center of the mall. In the corner of the screen, the Boosters began to build their pyramid. The music pounded, the crowd clapped. The camera swung upside down again, and a small, upside-down Jessica started running toward the pyramid.

Maria jumped when the TV boomed with the sound of breaking glass and then a shockingly loud alarm. Upside-down Jessica fuzzily leaped toward the toppling pyramid and dropped into a clumsy heap on the floor.

Maria heard Lila snickering in the darkness.

The screen went white with the column again, then the camera made a wobbling, swooping loop to the right. It was the broken window of Precious Stones jewelry store, out of focus and really shaky. People began to swarm toward the window—the grouchy security guard, the clown handing out balloons, a lady with a baby carriage . . .

Two more minutes passed of the same scene. Lila's family room was quiet. Maria wiped her eyes on her sleeve and tried to keep back a sniffle. Her movie was a disaster. Worse than a disaster. What had she been thinking? Why had she assumed she'd be good at this? It was the worst movie she had ever seen.

Everyone jumped when Jessica flicked the lights back on.

"Maria, did you deliberately set out to make the Boosters look totally stupid?" Jessica demanded.

Maria felt terrible. Terrible because she had let the Boosters down, and embarrassed that she had let herself down so badly. She must have been kidding herself. When she remembered how she had boasted that filmmaking was in her blood, she wanted to die.

"Yeah, Maria. That video was really important to us, and now you've ruined it," Janet said angrily.

"I didn't mean to—" Maria began.

"Maybe Maria was imitating a famous director's style," Melissa suggested calmly. "Like Fellini or somebody."

"Yeah. I mean—I don't know," Johanna said shyly. "It was kind of interesting. Maybe if it was edited, and had a cute sound track . . ."

"Get a clue, Johanna," Janet scoffed. "We don't have an audition video, and that's that."

Lila tossed her long brown hair over one shoulder. "The only thing good about that video is that you captured Jessica falling off the pyramid. That was pretty funny."

"There wasn't a pyramid to fall off of," Jessica

snapped, standing up to face Lila. "You had already fallen down yourselves!"

"Excuses, excuses," Lila said angrily.

Maria could tell that a real argument was about to break out. Maybe they would be so caught up fighting with one another that she could sneak out and go home—where she could destroy that awful tape forever.

Standing up quietly, she slipped over to Lila's VCR and popped the tape out. Lila and Jessica were still sniping at each other, and all the Boosters were taking sides. Maria shoved the tape into her bag and turned to slink out the door—only to run right into Elizabeth.

"Maria," Elizabeth said, patting her shoulder, "don't worry about the Boosters. You just need more practice with your camera, that's all."

Maria sighed. "I need more than practice, Elizabeth. I need to throw this camera in the garbage!"

Elizabeth took a quick look around the room, then grabbed Maria's arm and pulled her out into the hallway. They tiptoed to Lila's front door and quietly let themselves out.

"Look, Maria," Elizabeth said with a sigh. "No one can just pick up a camera and make a fabulous video the very first time. You need to practice with it. It's like when I got my new computer. I didn't even know how to turn it on. But now I'm used to it, and it's easy. This camera will be just the same, you'll see."

Maria appreciated what Elizabeth was trying to do, but it was obvious that she didn't know what she was talking about. The two girls walked home in silence.

"Round two of the best-Booster competition will now begin," Janet announced to the group gathered in Lila's backyard.

Lila was teetering precariously on the wooden fence that surrounded much of her vast lawn. Arms waving wildly, she walked a ten-foot length of it, then jumped down victoriously at the end.

"There, Miss Smarty," she gloated. "Let's see you do *that*. If you think you could have kept the pyramid up with your superhuman balance, then prove it." She shot Kimberly a triumphant smile.

Kimberly had come up with the idea for the fence-walking contest after Jessica had criticized the other Boosters' balance.

Glaring at Lila, Jessica stalked to the fence. Winston gave her a leg up, and she stood up slowly. The board she was on was only about three inches wide, and she was at least four feet off the ground. For a few moments she stood there shakily, trying to concentrate on getting her balance, and trying not to look at the ground, which seemed like a very long way away.

Jessica took one hesitant step, aware of all the Boosters watching her. This was so unfair—everyone knew she was a better Booster than Lila any day. If that stupid mall robbery hadn't taken place, none of this would be happening.

On the ground, Lila made a low "Bawk-awk-awk" sound like a chicken. That did it. Jessica set her jaw and took a step, then another. This was easy. No prob. She would show Lila, and all the rest of the Boosters, too. She was the better Booster. No question about it. She was by far the—

"Aiieee!" Jessica cried as her foot slipped. She wobbled horribly for a few long, terrifying moments, then she was falling with a heavy thud. "Ow! Oommph!" For a moment Jessica lay on the grass, trying to suck in some breath.

Grace ran over to her. "Jessica, are you OK?" she asked anxiously.

Jessica nodded, trying to speak, but no words came. Her shoulder hurt, and the ankle she had twisted earlier that day still throbbed gently. Above her, she saw Lila's smiling face looming.

"Lila, two; Jessica, zero," Lila said triumphantly.

Five

◇

"Do you think you can finish that article in time?" Sophia Rizzo asked Elizabeth on Monday. It was lunchtime, and Elizabeth was in the *Sweet Valley Sixers* office, working on her account of the mall robbery. She was feeling a little frazzled—besides this article about the robbery, she was going to do a piece about the Boosters' performance, not to mention the food-court review.

Elizabeth nodded. "I think so. There really isn't much to say. The newspapers haven't given any facts at all."

"You were there, weren't you?" Julie Porter asked. Julie was Johanna's sister and a fellow *Sixers* contributor. "Johanna and I were at the mall, but we were so far away we didn't even know what had happened."

"Maria and I were standing right there," Elizabeth said with a sigh. "But it must have been a really well-planned job. I whirled around as soon as I heard the glass breaking, and the burglar had already gotten away. I didn't see anyone running or hiding."

"It was really something," Amy agreed. She was the assistant editor of the paper. Humming along softly with the song on the radio, she rearranged photographs on a desktop, trying to decide on a composition.

Julie leaned over the school's computer, which they used to typeset their newspaper. They'd recently gotten brand-new software, which made the paper look more professional than ever.

The *Sixers* came out every Friday, so articles had to be finished by Tuesday morning if they were going to make it into the next issue. By Wednesday all the articles and photographs were in position in the computer program, and then on Thursday the papers were printed and stapled. On Friday they were distributed.

"Hmm. I have a small space left on this one page," Julie mused. "Sophia, could you hand me Bruce's review of his new tennis racket? I think I can cut it down to fit."

Sophia brought the article over. Besides the regular staff reporters and photographers, the *Sixers* also accepted guest articles, reviews, and photo essays. They saved them up, and when space permitted, fit them in.

Elizabeth looked up and grinned. "I can't believe we're using that. Isn't it just about how fabulous Bruce is, especially since he got his new racket?"

Julie smirked. "Yeah. It's pretty silly, but it's just the right length. No one takes Bruce seriously anyway."

"Except Bruce," Elizabeth reminded her with a laugh.

Bruce Patman was a seventh grader, and one of the richest kids at Sweet Valley Middle School. Elizabeth and all her friends thought he was amazingly snobby, stuck-up, and arrogant. She knew several girls, though, who thought he was adorable.

For the next few minutes each of the girls worked on her project quietly, while the radio played soft music.

"We're interrupting this program to bring you news of the latest theft at the Valley Mall," the radio newscaster suddenly announced.

Heads jerked up all over the newsroom, and Elizabeth stared at Amy in shock. Julie ran over to turn up the radio.

"A little more than an hour ago," the radio announcer said, "another store at the Valley Mall was robbed. Hello Again, a store that sells greeting cards, party decorations, and porcelain figurines, reported that their cash register was forced open and all their cash taken. Also stolen were some of their more expensive figurines and some costume jewelry. The theft occurred while the one salesperson ducked into the storeroom for a moment, she said."

"This is incredible," Elizabeth muttered. She glanced at the clock on the wall. Lunch period was almost over. She wanted to run over to the mall right away to look for clues or interview witnesses.

It was so frustrating to have to stay in school all afternoon.

"Apparently there were no witnesses," the announcer said. "We asked one of the security guards on duty, a Mr. Leonard MacDuff, what his impressions were. Mr. MacDuff?"

Elizabeth instantly recognized the gruff tones of the guard who had shooed her and Maria away from Precious Stones.

"It doesn't make sense," Mr. MacDuff growled. "I had just walked by there on my regular rounds, and I didn't see or hear anything unusual. It must be some kind of inside job."

Elizabeth snorted. "Didn't see or hear anything! What kind of guard is he? He was right by Precious Stones when it got robbed, and he didn't see anything then, either."

"Maybe it *is* an inside job," Amy speculated. "The mall is always so full of people, I don't know how anyone could pull it off."

"Pull what off?" Todd Wilkins asked, coming into the newsroom. Todd was a sixth grader and the star of the middle school basketball team. He and Elizabeth had been good friends for years, and lately they had started to seem like more than that.

"The latest robbery at the mall," Julie said, filling him in. "Another store got robbed, just a little while ago."

"Wow. Two stores in three days. It must be a gang. I was going to go to the mall this afternoon. That's why I stopped by, Elizabeth. Want to come?"

"Yeah! That's a great idea. I need to review another food place anyway. While we're at the mall, maybe I could look around a little," Elizabeth said excitedly, hoping she might notice something that the police hadn't seen yet.

"Cool. So I'll meet you in front of school after last period." Todd smiled at her as he left the newsroom.

He has a really nice smile, Elizabeth thought. Then her mind snapped into mystery-solving gear. "Amy," she said, "can you meet me and Todd at the mall today? We should get Maria, too."

"Um, Elizabeth," Amy said, looking hesitant. "I'm not sure we should get tangled up in this. Maybe we should just leave it to the police."

"Amy, you heard the guy on the radio. The police don't know anything. Come on—it won't hurt to just look around a little. Just pretend we're going to the mall to hang out. We'll be very casual."

Amy sighed. "OK. I'll ask Maria to meet us at the food court after school. I don't know if she'll want to come. She's keeping a pretty low profile since the video disaster."

"It'll be good for her," Elizabeth said firmly. "I'll see you guys there."

"Wow, how many is that?" Janet asked in a low voice.

Tamara checked her score pad. "Twelve."

"This is pretty awesome," Winston said. "I don't think I've ever seen anything like it. How did you come up with this idea, Mandy?"

Mandy Miller smiled and shrugged. "I don't know. Somehow, with Jessica and Lila, it just seemed to make sense."

A group of kids were gathered around the Unicorner, which was the special table that the Unicorns had claimed for their own in the school cafeteria.

Lila and Jessica sat across from each other at the table, a large bowl of green grapes between them.

Very slowly and deliberately, Jessica reached out, plucked a grape from the bunch, and pushed it into her already totally bulging cheeks.

"Thirteen," Tamara said crisply, marking it down on her score pad.

"This is kind of dumb, if you ask me," Kimberly Haver said with a sniff. "What do grapes have to do with being a good Booster?"

"Nothing," Winston said. "But you can get Lila and Jessica to compete over anything."

Jessica steadfastly ignored the chatter around her. It was taking all her concentration to relax her face muscles and remember not to chew. She shifted some grapes around in her mouth experimentally. It felt as though she could fit two, maybe three more. *I can't believe Lila has kept up with me so far. I never would have thought her little ferret face would hold so many grapes.*

Across from her, Lila pushed another grape into her mouth. Her cheeks were huge and taut, and a thin stream of grape juice began to trickle down her chin. Jessica noted that Lila was beginning to look a little green herself.

"Lila, thirteen," Tamara said as she made a note on the pad.

"Is someone getting a picture of this?" Mandy asked, laughing.

Keeping her eyes locked on Lila's, Jessica picked up another grape and carefully wedged it into a little pocket of space inside her cheek. She felt as though she might choke to death. *Breathe through your nose. Relax. You have this in the bag, she told herself.*

A low murmur of approval came from the crowd.

"Jessica, fourteen," Tamara whispered.

"I can't stand the suspense," Winston said, biting his knuckles.

Lila's nostrils were flaring, and her mouth was white around its tightly stretched edges. Jessica felt a tingle of anticipation as she saw the look of rising panic in Lila's eyes. *She can't do it. She's gonna crack. Hold steady, Jess. Victory will be yours.*

Then Lila's eyes hardened again, and almost too quickly she reached out for another grape. The crowd gasped. Lila's cheeks were packed so full of grapes, she looked as though she were playing an invisible trumpet. She just barely managed to fit another grape into her mouth, although she almost had to hold it in place with her hand. Her mouth was so full, she couldn't keep her lips closed.

"Lila, fourteen."

Jessica's eyes narrowed. Right at that moment, she would have given anything to be able to force her teeth together, crush some grapes, swallow some juice, and be able to close her mouth again. Or else to spit out her mouthful of grapes. She was tired of breathing grape fumes. Tired of the insistent trickle of grape juice down the back of her throat. Tired of the smooth, sticky feel of grapes in her hand. But she couldn't let Lila win. She was going to win this grape-eating contest or die in the attempt.

She took another grape. In the crowd gathered around their table, eyes widened, breaths were drawn. Everyone remained very, very still.

She pushed the grape in.

The crowd let out its breath.

Tamara looked as though she couldn't believe it.

"Jessica, fifteen," she said in an awestruck voice, marking it down.

Lila looked outraged. Her eyes bugged out and her hands clenched on the tabletop. Suddenly she leaned forward and opened her mouth.

"Aiiieee!" someone in the crowd cried.

"Ewwwwwww," Tamara said, looking away.

"Whoa," Ken Matthews said, staring in horrified fascination.

A flood of partially crushed green grapes spilled out of Lila's mouth onto her lunch tray.

"Pretty disgusting," Winston commented, taking a bite of his apple.

Sweet, sweet success, Jessica thought in triumph. Using all her strength, she slowly chomped down through her grapes until finally her teeth met again. Then she began to swallow a little bit at a time until she could chew normally. She really felt as though she might barf at any second.

"Well," Tamara said, "this round definitely goes to Jessica. The best-Booster score so far is Lila, two; Jessica, one."

"I don't care," Lila panted in a raspy voice. "Of course she would win, with that *big mouth of hers.*"

Jessica managed a grapey grin. She was still swallowing. With any luck at all, she would never have to see, smell, or be around green grapes for the rest of her life.

"Hmm, this is great," Amy said appreciatively, slurping up the last of her banana smoothie. She, Maria, Elizabeth, and Todd were all sitting at a little white iron table at Smootharama at the mall's sparkling new food court.

"Yeah," Maria agreed, pushing her glass away. "I definitely recommend the strawberry."

Elizabeth noticed that Maria still seemed sad and withdrawn about her video. When Elizabeth had tried to talk to her about it, Maria had said the subject was closed. Elizabeth hoped she would get over it soon, and that she wouldn't give up film-making forever.

"My mango-pineapple one was awesome," Todd said. He frowned. "I wonder if I have room for one more."

"Todd!" Elizabeth looked up from her notepad with a smile. "Only you could have two smoothies after school and not ruin your dinner."

"Hey—*nothing* ruins my dinner," Todd protested. "I'm a growing boy."

Laughing, Elizabeth turned back to her notes. "OK. Now, I'm just trying to write down my impressions and any facts we can find." For a moment she looked up and scanned the mall.

"The mood at the mall seemed a little subdued," she said, writing it down in her notepad. "Several stores have hired extra security guards." She looked up again. "What have you guys noticed? Tell me your impressions, and I'll write them down."

Amy and Maria looked at each other. Todd was thoughtfully licking the spoon of his mango-pineapple smoothie.

"Elizabeth, we wanted to talk to you about that," Amy started. Maria nodded.

"We've been thinking, and we feel—well, as though we're just not sure we want to get mixed up in another mystery."

"We got in a lot of trouble last time," Maria reminded Elizabeth softly. "And you practically got yourself killed. We want to be supportive, but maybe you should just stick to reporting this one, instead of trying to solve it."

Elizabeth stared at Maria, wide-eyed. "Maria, doesn't it drive you crazy that we were right there at the first robbery and still didn't see anything? Aren't you dying to know what kind of crook could pull something like that off? Wouldn't you love to be a local hero by solving the crime that's stumped the police?"

"Well, no," Maria admitted.

"Me, neither. I'm sorry," Amy said.

Maria shrugged. "I mean, I do think it's really interesting. I have to admit I am curious about this. But it might just be too dangerous for us," Maria argued.

"My parents would kill me," Amy added.

Elizabeth sat back in her chair, feeling disappointed. Her friends had a point, but still—she just didn't understand how they could let this opportunity pass them by. "OK. It's OK," she said finally. "I wouldn't want you guys to get into trouble."

Maria and Amy looked relieved. "Great," Amy said. "I really better be going. I'll talk to you later, OK?"

"OK."

Maria decided to take the bus home with Amy, and a few moments later Elizabeth and Todd were alone at their table.

"Hey, you want to go to Sound Trek?" Todd asked after he'd finished his second smoothie. "I want to look at some new headphones."

"Sure," Elizabeth said, shutting her notepad. "Maybe I'll look around a little on the way."

As they walked to Sound Trek, however, Elizabeth had to admit that the mall looked very much as usual. There were a few extra security guards standing conspicuously in front of stores, pacing back and forth, but other than that, it was the same old Valley Mall. Even the pane of glass at Precious Stones had already been replaced.

"So what are you looking for?" Todd asked as they walked. "Maybe I can help."

Elizabeth smiled at him gratefully. "I don't even know," she confessed. "Clues, suspicious behavior . . . I feel like I should recognize some pattern, something that would tip me off."

"Do you think there are going to be more burglaries?"

Elizabeth frowned. "I don't know. I hope not, but somehow I can't help thinking there are."

At Sound Trek, they wandered over to the headphones section and Todd started trying on different pairs.

A young sales assistant came over. "Can I help you?" he asked pleasantly.

Todd stepped forward. "Yes. I need a new pair of headphones. How's this brand?" He held up the most comfortable pair he had tried.

Elizabeth stood back, watching absentmindedly, waiting for Todd to be done. *That guy's kind of funny-looking,* she thought, watching the salesclerk.

Soon Todd had decided, and they walked over to the counter to pay. Todd handed over his money, and the salesclerk took it. Something about his hand caught Elizabeth's eye. *What a weird scar. I wonder how he got it.* The salesclerk had a long, pink scar running across the back of his hand.

"Cool!" Todd said to Elizabeth as they walked out of the store.

"Do you like them?" she asked.

"Yeah. They have separate controls on each side, so you can adjust the volume, and they're really comfortable. Do you want to try them?"

"No, thanks," Elizabeth said, laughing. "Not unless they help me hear some clues."

Six

◇

"Ready, set, go!" Steven yelled, then hit his stopwatch. It was Tuesday afternoon, and he was standing by the Wakefields' pool in their backyard.

Jessica and Lila dove into the water and began swimming across the length of the pool.

"Go, Lila!" Janet screamed from the sidelines.

"Go, Jessica!" Amy yelled.

"Another day, another contest, huh?" Elizabeth asked, walking across the patio to the sliding kitchen doors.

"Uh-huh," Amy answered. She grinned. "I'm here in my official Booster capacity. In fact, this swimming contest was my idea."

"I see," Elizabeth said. She shifted her schoolbooks to the other hip. "What's the deal this time?"

"The most number of laps in five minutes," Amy replied.

In the sparkling blue water of the pool, Jessica

and Lila tapped the opposite end and began to stroke their way back across.

"And that's one!" Steven yelled, glancing at his stopwatch. "Four minutes, forty-five seconds to go!"

Elizabeth rolled her eyes. "When is this going to end? Someone's going to end up getting hurt or something."

Tamara, standing nearby, nodded. "The grape episode yesterday was *not* pretty."

Shaking her head, Elizabeth headed for the kitchen, and Amy followed her. Jessica had been too nauseated to eat dinner the night before and had had a stomachache most of the night. Elizabeth didn't know how Jessica had dragged herself through a whole day of school today, let alone gotten into a laps contest.

"And that's five!" Steven shouted. "Jessica Wakefield is in the lead!"

Tamara, Kimberly, Mary, Grace, Mandy, and Janet continued to cheer on the sidelines, evenly divided for Jessica or Lila.

"Lila said she'd bought a new racer swimsuit just for this race," Janet said. "I think she's going to win."

"You're only saying that because she's your cousin," Grace said. "Jessica is doing really well."

"We'll see who comes out on top," Kimberly sneered.

"And that's eleven!" Steven yelled. "Won't be long now, folks."

Two minutes later, Steven was kneeling at the deep end of the pool as Lila plowed forward and tapped the brick edging.

"We have a winner," Steven said somewhat un-enthusiastically. "Lila Fowler, with twenty-seven laps in five minutes."

Lila clung limply to the side of the pool, barely keeping her head above water.

Jessica swam up a few seconds later and brushed the bricks with the prunelike tips of her fingers. "No . . . f-fair," she panted in an almost inaudible gasp. "I have a cramp. I . . . insist on a . . . rematch." She held on to the bricks with three fingers, looking pale and cold and pathetic.

"Rematch, my butt," Lila snarled weakly. "I won fair and square. The score is now Lila, three; Jessica, one. I think it's pretty clear who's the better Booster." She rested her head against the side of the pool, still breathing hard, water dripping out of her long brown hair.

"But you had a new racer swimsuit," Jessica complained. "That . . . gave you an unfair . . . advantage. Give me a day to go shopping, then . . . we'll see who really . . . should have won."

Shakily, Lila heaved herself out of the pool and lay on the warm patio pavement. Janet ran over and covered her with a towel. Kimberly gave her a sip of orange juice.

"The only advantage I have, Jessica Wakefield," Lila muttered, "is that I'm not absolutely *nuts*, like you are!" She crawled to her hands and knees, then Janet helped her up. Lila stomped angrily toward the house to change.

Mary and Grace gave Jessica sympathetic glances. "I really better get going, Jess," Mary said.

"I'll see you tomorrow, OK? It was a good race. You'll get her next time."

Grace said good-bye, too, mumbling something about homework, and they let themselves out the patio gate.

"Steven, I can't get out," Jessica said in a small voice, still clutching the edge of the pool like a sodden, bedraggled rag.

"Sure you can. Come on, Jess," Steven said briskly.

"I can't," Jessica insisted feebly. "I don't have the strength. I'm going to drown here, like a total loser." She sank a little lower in the water and started to sniffle sadly.

"Dog-paddle to the steps," he advised.

"I can't."

Steven stood there, looking down at his younger sister. When she wanted to, Jessica could look very pitiful. She was looking that way now. He sighed, then looked toward the house. Lila must have gone out the front door, he figured. He couldn't believe that skinny little weasel had beaten Jessica. Jessica was usually so tough. Another damp sniffle came out of the pool behind him.

He sighed again, then stripped off his shirt and pushed off his sneakers. "OK, Jess, hang on," he said, walking over to the steps of the pool.

"Thank you, Steven," came Jessica's frail little voice.

Steven splashed into the water, then swam over to Jessica. "Hold on to my shoulders," he instructed. She gave him a tiny waterlogged smile and transferred her grip from the bricks.

He swam slowly back to the steps, pretending he was a shark with a barnacle stuck to his back.

After dinner, Elizabeth was in her room, working on her food-court review. "In this reporter's opinion, the coconut-orange smoothie was a platonic experience: a full, richly satisfying taste sensation, with the milky, heavier, pure coconut flavor balanced subtly by the fresh, tart citrusness of the fresh-squeezed orange juice. . . ."

Elizabeth paused. *Citrusness? Citrusion? Citrosity?* She heard a tap on her door.

"Elizabeth? Phone." It was her mom.

"Thanks, Mom." She went to answer the hall extension. "Hello?"

"Elizabeth? Hey. It's Todd. Can you come meet me at the mall?"

"What? We were just there. Anyway, it's a school night, and I have a lot of work to do."

Todd paused. "Oh. I just thought you might want to come."

Elizabeth frowned into the phone. Who did he think she was, Ken Matthews? A girl liked to have a little advance warning. A girl liked to feel that she wasn't being taken for granted. A girl liked it when a boy called up just to—

"I mean, with the latest robbery and all," Todd said. "But if you're busy, I guess—"

"*What?*" Elizabeth screeched.

Ten minutes later Elizabeth raced into the mall after locking her bicycle to a post outside.

She met Todd by the center fountain.

"I got here as fast as I could," she said, panting. "Now, what happened? Tell me everything. Hi, Ken."

Ken Matthews said hello back and grinned at her.

"Well, we didn't actually see the robbery," Todd told her. He sounded disappointed.

Elizabeth whipped out her notepad and started writing. "Uh-huh, go on."

"We were playing video games in the arcade."

"Wait," Elizabeth commanded. "What store was actually robbed?"

"That's what I wanted to tell you," Todd said excitedly. "It was that electronics store, Sound Trek."

Elizabeth gasped. It was the second robbery that had taken place practically right in front of her face! "When did it happen?"

"About an hour ago. We were at the arcade—"

"I was whipping Todd at Spacefighter," Ken said helpfully. "Write that down."

"Yeah, Ken was *cheating* at Spacefighter, and then all of a sudden we noticed cops running by. We followed them and saw they were swarming all over the electronics store. Then someone in the crowd said that it had been robbed. So I ran and called you."

Elizabeth gave him a big smile and squeezed his hand. "Thanks, Todd. I really appreciate it. Let's go take a look."

They walked down the wide mall corridor to the wing where Sound Trek was located. As Todd had said, policemen and policewomen were all over the place, talking into walkie-talkies. Startled shoppers had crowded around the store's entrance, which had its metal security gate pulled down.

Elizabeth pushed past a clown and a person wearing a Chicken Lickin' uniform to try to get closer to the store. Although she could see through the metal gate, the store didn't look any different from how it had looked this afternoon. Nothing was knocked over, there were no signs of a struggle.

"OK, now, everybody clear out. Let the police do their job."

Elizabeth instantly recognized Mr. MacDuff, the grumpy security guard. *No wonder he's so mean,* Elizabeth thought. *Three stores have been robbed, and he's supposed to be guarding them!*

A policeman came up to Mr. MacDuff.

"How long have you been on duty, sir?" he asked. "Were you here about an hour ago?"

Mr. MacDuff shook his head. "Just came on at eight o'clock. Today's usually my day off, but they called me to come in because Joe's sick."

Elizabeth ducked behind a column and scribbled furiously, trying to write down every word of their conversation.

"Who's Joe?" the cop asked.

"Joe Winston. He's another security guard. Today's his day, but he called in sick," Mr. MacDuff explained grumpily.

"OK. We may need to question you more later," the policeman told the guard. "You'll be around for a while, right?"

"Yeah, I'll be here." MacDuff turned to the crowd. "Come on, now, everybody. Let's give the police some room. Go on and finish up your shopping."

This is unbelievable, Elizabeth thought. *It's a real crime wave, right here in the Valley Mall. And it all started the day Maria was making her movie of the Boosters.*

Elizabeth looked through the crowd and found a policeman. "Excuse me, sir," she said. "My name is Elizabeth Wakefield."

The cop looked down at her. "Were you here just now, when Sound Trek was robbed?"

"No," Elizabeth said. "But I was here earlier this afternoon. And I was at the first robbery, the one at Precious Stones. My friend Maria and I were right there. Maria was making a video of the Boosters." She smiled ruefully. "Actually, she ended up making a video of the entire mall, but that's another story."

Giving her a patient look, the cop said, "Uh-huh?"

"Well, I was just wondering if I could take a look at the police reports—you know, compare notes. Since I've been close to two of the robberies."

The cop pushed his blue cap back. "Well, miss, I have to tell you that we don't allow civilians access to our reports until the crimes have been solved. I'm sorry."

"But I'm a reporter for *The Sweet Valley Sixers,*" Elizabeth pointed out. "My school newspaper at Sweet Valley Middle School. Could I see the reports in an official capacity?"

"Sorry, kid. You'll have to wait like everyone else." The cop looked apologetic.

"OK," Elizabeth said reluctantly.

"But if you or your friend remember anything

you think the police should know about the first robbery, you call us, OK?"

"Don't you want our names?" Elizabeth persisted.

"Oh, OK," the cop said, taking out a small notepad.

Elizabeth gave him her and Maria's names and addresses.

"OK, Elizabeth, thanks for your interest." The policeman smiled at her and moved back toward his partner.

The crowd began to disperse. Todd, Elizabeth, and Ken decided they had seen about all there was to see.

"Do you have time for a snack?" Todd asked.

"Well, I do need to review another food-court restaurant," Elizabeth said. "Maybe if we make it really fast. My mom said not to be too long, since it's a school night."

On their way through the crowd, she bumped into the young guy wearing the Chicken Lickin' uniform.

"Oh, excuse me," she said, looking up into his face.

"That's OK," he said with a smile. "No harm done."

He looked oddly familiar, and Elizabeth frowned, trying to remember.

"Hey, aren't you the guy who waited on me today in Sound Trek?" Todd asked him.

The guy pushed his Chicken Lickin' paper hat back on his head and looked at Todd. Then he smiled and snapped his fingers. "Yeah, you're right!" he said. "A pair of earphones, right?"

"Right," Todd said, looking pleased. "But how come you're wearing a Chicken Lickin' uniform now?"

"I'll tell you," the guy said. "It was a stroke of luck.

Today was my last day at Sound Trek. Chicken Lickin' actually offered me more money—can you believe it? So I left Sound Trek at five and started my new job. And a good thing, too. I mean, I'd hate to have been the guy on duty when the place was robbed." He pretended to shiver. "They say the guy actually had a gun."

"A gun!" Elizabeth exclaimed.

"Yeah. Of course, that's only what I heard," the guy said quickly. "I could be wrong. But I heard that he made the clerk go into the closet—at gunpoint—and stay there while he robbed the place. Pretty creepy, huh?"

"Yeah," Todd agreed, looking solemn.

"Well, you take care," the guy said. "And be careful around this mall. There's obviously a maniac running loose."

"OK, we will," Elizabeth said.

After the guy left, Todd turned to Elizabeth with wide eyes. "Wow. That guy was lucky to get out when he did."

"*We* were really lucky—it got robbed only a couple hours after we left," Elizabeth reminded him.

"Well, let's go to the Dog House," Ken suggested, "and see if it gets robbed while we're there."

"Ken!" Elizabeth laughed. "What kind of thief would rob a hot-dog place?"

Ken thought for a moment. "A cat burglar?"

Elizabeth and Todd looked at each other.

"Get him!" Todd cried, and he and Elizabeth started pummeling Ken right in the middle of the food court.

Seven

◇

"So I guess these articles won't go in this week's paper," Julie Porter told Elizabeth. It was Wednesday morning, and Elizabeth had stopped by the *Sixers* office before homeroom.

Elizabeth sighed. "Not the mall-robberies one," she admitted. "It isn't close to being finished. There are still too many loose ends and no solution. But I can give you my review of the first three food places: Taco Shack, Smootharama, and the Dog House." She pulled the article out of her backpack.

Julie counted how many words the piece contained. "I think we can just fit it in on the second-to-last page. Let me have the disk."

Elizabeth gave Julie the disk of the article, and Julie put it into the school's computer. She called up the file and quickly chose a typeface and size. After Julie hit a few buttons, Elizabeth watched her article transform into two neat columns of the newspaper's typeface.

"That is so cool," she said. "You're a whiz with this computer, Julie."

"It's our new software program," Julie said modestly. "Now we need a title. How about 'Where to Go and What to Eat'?"

Elizabeth nodded approvingly. "Good. It's short, snappy, and to the point."

Julie typed it in, then made it appear in larger letters over the two columns. Later, she would electronically paste the article into position on its page, and the whole page would be printed.

"Maybe you should read it and see if you can tighten it up any," Elizabeth suggested. "I wrote it pretty quickly last night, after I got back from the mall."

"OK. Let's see . . . 'The Taco Shack, while not offering a new or interesting interpretation of the taco, does fill a gap in the food-court menu selection,'" Julie read. "'The Valley Mall has long ignored our neighbors south of the border in its restaurant offerings, and this reporter, for one, is glad that Latino cuisine is finally being represented.'" Julie looked up admiringly. "This is great, Elizabeth. I can't wait to read the others. Why don't we give each restaurant a little symbol, like they do in the big newspapers. You know, four stars if it's good or no stars if it's bad."

"That's a great idea!" Elizabeth said enthusiastically. "What symbol should we choose?"

"Let me see what the computer has already."

Julie called up a menu on her screen. "This one is perfect," she said, pointing to the screen. The symbol was a small fist with its thumb sticking up. "See? You could give it two thumbs up, or three, or one, or even a thumbs-down if the place is bad."

"Perfect!" Elizabeth agreed. "OK. Give Smootharama four thumbs up. Taco Shack gets two and a half. The Dog House gets three."

"OK. I'll take care of it."

"Great." Elizabeth slung her backpack over her shoulder. "Now, if I can just solve the great mall mystery, my life as a reporter will be complete."

Suddenly Amy appeared in the doorway to the *Sixers* office, shaking her head in disapproval.

"I know, I know," Elizabeth said. "Don't even say it, Amy."

"Jessica, why don't you just give up now," Lila said impatiently.

Jessica twisted sideways to look at Lila. Lila, like Jessica, was hanging upside down from her knees on the monkey bars in the school yard. It was lunchtime, and they had been hanging there for almost ten minutes. Jessica was glad she hadn't eaten lunch yet.

Most days, the Unicorns felt that they were far too cool to spend time on the playground equipment—only boys and geeky girls did that. Unicorns usually sat and gossiped, or sometimes looked at fashion magazines, or listened to the latest Johnny Buck tape during lunch.

But today was different. Today Jessica had to

make up for bringing shame to the name of Wakefield. Today Jessica had to hang upside down from the monkey bars for the longest time or move out of town.

She looked at Lila again. Lila's face was bright pink, and her brown hair was hanging straight down almost to the ground. Lila was wearing white jeans and a purple T-shirt that she had knotted tightly at her waist so that it wouldn't fall down around her shoulders. Her dangling earrings were hanging down by the sides of her head.

Jessica giggled. Her knees hurt, and her feet were totally numb. She felt as though she would have abnormally long legs when this was over. All the blood had rushed to her head, and her face felt weird and full. Even her eyeballs felt heavy and strange. But still, Lila looked so funny, it almost cracked Jessica up.

"You don't exactly look like a model yourself," Lila sneered, seeming to know what Jessica had been thinking. "In fact, your face kind of looks like a pig, with long blond hair."

"In that case we must be twins," Jessica snapped. Then her vision was obscured by a pair of slim, tan knees right in front of her eyes.

"Sad to say, Jess, you already have a twin. Although I'm not sure I should admit that right now."

Jessica curled up enough to look into Elizabeth's face. Her sister looked mildly disapproving, but then, Elizabeth often looked mildly disapproving when Jessica was around.

"How long have you two been doing your bat imitation?" Elizabeth asked.

Janet checked her watch. "Eleven minutes, three seconds."

"And how long will you stay that way?"

"For as long as it takes," Jessica vowed through gritted teeth.

"Hey, maybe I should write an article about this for the *Sixers*," Elizabeth said, perking up. "You guys just *hang around* for a minute while I go get a camera."

"Elizabeth Wakefield, don't you dare," Lila said. "I would never, ever forgive you."

"I agree with ferret-face," Jessica said. "Butt out, Elizabeth. No pictures are allowed. Go help an old lady cross the street or something."

Elizabeth walked away, laughing and shaking her head.

"Your sister is really sick sometimes," Lila said. "Janet, how long has it been now?"

"Fourteen minutes, thirty seconds."

Lila sighed and shifted uncomfortably. "I think gangrene is setting in below my knees."

"I thought it was in your head," Jessica countered.

Lila twisted angrily and glared at her. "Shut up! Ow!" She reached up and rubbed her knees, but the motion caused her to slip a little. Panicking, she tightened her grip on the metal bar, but it was too late. With an outraged shriek, she fell heavily to the ground.

"Yes!" Jessica punched the air, then grabbed her metal bar and slowly lowered herself to the ground. "Yes! Let the record show that Jessica won this event! The score is now three–two!"

She wobbled around victoriously, then looked uncertain and kind of alarmed.

"I think the score is Lila, lame; Jessica, green. You better sit down," Grace Oliver said, taking Jessica's arm and pushing her to a bench.

"I think maybe I stood up too soon," Jessica moaned. "All the blood rushed back down to my feet. I'm going to faint."

Grace helped Jessica lean over with her head between her knees as Jessica prayed silently not to throw up. It had been the same way with those dumb grapes, she thought miserably. She had won, but she had almost hurled in the process. Couldn't she, just once, win some contest that didn't involve extreme queasiness?

Lila came to sit beside her on the bench. "The score's still three–two, you know," Lila said wearily. "We should have one more event, and then, after I win, the contest will be over."

"If I win, we'll have to have a tiebreaker," Jessica mumbled, her head still between her knees.

"But you won't," Lila said, rubbing her hand across her forehead. "So let's make the prize a little sweeter. The winner of the best-Booster contest not only gets first pick at our costumes on Saturday but from now on also gets to be on top of the Booster pyramid."

Jessica's head snapped up in horror. "No way! I'm always on top of the pyramid!"

Lila smirked, her face slowly returning to its normal color. "Not if you don't win."

Jessica looked horrified for a moment, then bit

her lip. "OK," she snapped. "Fine. But you'll be sorry when you have to be on the bottom of the pyramid for the rest of your life!"

Lila pretended to yawn. "Hardly for the rest of my life, Jessica. Probably just till we graduate from middle school." She gave Jessica one last derogatory glance, then stood and sauntered away. She only wobbled a little bit.

Jessica bit the edge of her thumb, thinking hard. She had to win the contest tomorrow—no matter what. No way was she going to be on the bottom of the pyramid from now on. No way, no how.

"Maria, wait up!" Elizabeth ran after her friend. The final bell had just rung.

Maria turned and looked at Elizabeth quizzically. "What's up?"

"I've been looking for you all day," Elizabeth said. "I wanted to ask you about something. Can I come home with you this afternoon?"

"Sure. But why?"

"I'll tell you when we get to your house," Elizabeth said, shifting her backpack to her other shoulder. She wasn't sure how Maria would react, but last night she had decided to ask Maria to make a video record of all the exits of the mall. Maybe by studying them, she could figure out how the thief was coming and going. At any rate, she hoped it might cheer Maria up about her filmmaking skills.

"Can you just give me a hint?" Maria asked.

Elizabeth's eyes twinkled. "It has to do with your video camera."

Maria groaned. "Not that again, Elizabeth! I don't want to talk about it. It's obvious I was kidding myself about being a filmmaker. I'll just stick to being a has-been actress," she said forlornly.

"Maria, stop that!" Elizabeth exclaimed. "You haven't even given filmmaking a chance. And you're *not* a has-been actress. You have a whole career ahead of you. You'll realize that as soon as you stop feeling sorry for yourself."

Maria couldn't help grinning. "Yes, Mom."

Elizabeth laughed, then paused in her tracks, a concerned expression on her face. "Maria, is Nina already home from school?" she asked.

They were standing on the walkway leading to Maria's house. Elizabeth pointed to the front door, which was slightly ajar.

Maria quickly turned to look in the driveway. Neither of her parents' cars was home. "Nina!" she yelled, stepping hesitantly to the front door. There was no answer. She gingerly pushed the front door open farther. Then the two girls' eyes widened, and they stared at each other.

From where she stood, Elizabeth could see past the foyer, into the living room. It looked as though a tornado had swept through the house. Sofa cushions were scattered around, and some of them had been ripped open. Books had been pulled out of the bookcases and were strewn around the floor. Vases had been knocked over, pictures yanked down from walls, and chairs pushed over and thrown out into the hall.

"We've been robbed," Maria whispered, her voice shaking.

*   *   *

That night after dinner, the phone rang, and Steven ran to get it.

"Yes? Wakefield Insane Asylum," he said casually. "Oh, hi, Maria. Yeah, Elizabeth's here. Where else would she be? It's not like she has a social life. Are you sure you want to talk to her? Why don't you just talk with me instead, heh heh heh . . . Ouch!"

Elizabeth grabbed the phone and punched Steven in the arm. "You are so immature," she hissed.

Steven sauntered back to the kitchen table, where he was met by a cool look from his mother.

"Steven, I do *not* want you answering the phone with 'Wakefield Insane Asylum.' What if that had been a client of mine or your father's?"

"OK, OK," Steven grumbled. "No one in this house has a sense of humor."

Elizabeth put the phone down on the counter. "Hang it up when I get upstairs, OK?"

"Hello, Maria?" she said when she'd reached the upstairs phone. "Are you all right? What happened?"

After the girls had found Maria's house broken into, they had run to a neighbor's to call the police and Maria's parents. Elizabeth had stayed with Maria next door until they had seen the cops arrive, and shortly after that, Nina and Maria's parents had come home.

"Well, after you left, the cops went through the house to make sure no one was still there."

Elizabeth shivered. "Uh-huh."

"They said we'd done the right thing by not going inside," Maria continued. "Then my parents and I went in. The weird thing was, only the living room and the family room were messed up. All the other rooms were fine."

"Did they take the TVs? Your mom's jewelry? The silver?"

"Well, we're still going through everything and comparing it with the household list, for insurance. But so far, nothing like that seems to have been taken. It's really weird. It's almost like they were looking for something."

A chill went down Elizabeth's spine. "It's a good thing no one was home," she said shakily. "Do you think maybe it was the same person who's been doing the mall robberies?"

"Who knows? But it doesn't make sense. Why would they suddenly burgle a private house instead of the mall? And then not take the valuables? Anyway, my parents are pretty freaked out about it. My mom says she's going to leave work early tomorrow, so that I won't come home to an empty house."

"Good idea," Elizabeth agreed. "At least until they find the person who did it. So wasn't *anything* taken?"

"Not really. I mean, so far, the only things missing are all of our videotapes. Isn't that weird? I mean, what kind of thief breaks into a house and steals their copies of *Gone With the Wind* and *Roots* and *The Sound of Music*?"

"I don't know," Elizabeth said, her mind racing. "I mean, that's so weird. Why would anyone want a video? It doesn't make sense."

Eight

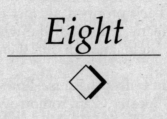

That night, long after everyone was in bed, Elizabeth lay on her stomach under the covers, re-reading everything she had ever written on the crime spree. Her flashlight was propped against her left shoulder so she could see.

When someone tapped her on the shoulder, she gasped and jumped about a foot in the air. A hand clamped tightly over her mouth to prevent her from calling out. Elizabeth struggled violently, but she was tangled in her sheet. Her panicked mind was whirling. The thief had come after her!

"Elizabeth, would you stop kicking me!" Jessica whispered.

As soon as she heard her sister's voice, Elizabeth went limp. When she had caught her breath again, she untangled herself from the covers and sat up.

"You almost gave me a heart attack!" she accused Jessica. "What are you doing up so late?"

"What are *you* doing up so late?" Jessica asked.

"I'm just trying to figure out what's going on. First the robberies at the mall, then Maria's house. I'm getting scared."

Jessica crawled into bed next to Elizabeth and sat with her back propped against the wall. Faint moonlight streamed through the window, making it just barely light enough for them to see each other.

"Well, *I* can't sleep because I'm worried about the final best-Booster event tomorrow," Jessica confessed. "I'll just die if Lila wins and gets to be on top of the Booster pyramid from now on."

Elizabeth patted her shoulder sympathetically. "You haven't been having very good luck with this contest so far," she said. "But maybe that'll change tomorrow. Just concentrate on whatever you're going to do, and try not to let Lila rattle you. Just tell yourself you can do it."

Jessica sighed. "That's what I've *been* doing, and so far I've hurt my shoulder, twisted my ankle, almost thrown up at school *twice*, and practically drowned myself. Who knows what'll happen tomorrow? And I have to win the tiebreaker, too."

Elizabeth tried not to smile. "Just do your best. Try not to worry about it too much."

"Oh, let's change the subject," Jessica said. "Tell me about the mall robberies."

"There's not much to tell," Elizabeth admitted.

"So what's the pattern with them? There's always a pattern," Jessica said knowledgeably.

"That's just it," Elizabeth said in frustration. "I

can't really find one. They occurred at different times of the day, in different sections of the mall. Each place robbed was a different type of business. Different things were taken each time—not just money." She paused, looking thoughtful.

"You need someone who could come and go at the mall all the time, without being noticed," Jessica mused. "Like a cleaning lady or something." She picked up Elizabeth's notes and read through them. Then she flipped back a few pages to reread a certain section. Quickly she ran her finger down another page, thumping it excitedly.

"Elizabeth! I can't believe you didn't see this!"

"What? What are you talking about?" Elizabeth leaned over Jessica's shoulder and tried to read where she was pointing.

"You *have* a pattern here," Jessica crowed. "It's right here in black and white. Or at least, blue and white. I can't believe you, with all your Amanda Howard mysteries, didn't spot this immediately, while I, who don't even like mysteries, took one look and—"

"Jessica, just tell me what you saw!"

"Don't you see the one name that keeps coming up in all your notes? *Mr. MacDuff!* It's MacDuff, MacDuff, MacDuff, all over the place. Look, he didn't want Maria and you to be too close to Precious Stones for the first robbery. He was interviewed right after the second robbery, but he said he didn't see a thing. For the third one, he says he just came on duty, but he could have been there for who knows how long. No one would notice him—

he's a *security guard*. He can come and go wherever and whenever he wants."

Elizabeth stared down at her notes, then up at Jessica. A glow came over her face. "Oh, my gosh, Jess—you may be right. He *is* the one consistent thing at all these robberies!"

Jessica blew on her fingernails and rubbed them across the top of her nightgown. "No, no—don't thank me. Just doing my job. I can't help it if I have amazing powers of observation and detection. I can't help it if I—"

"Oh, my gosh, Jess," Elizabeth said again, a horrified expression on her face. "I think I know why Maria's house got robbed. And I think it was my fault!"

The doorbell rang just as Maria's family was sitting down to breakfast on Thursday morning.

Mr. Slater frowned. "Who could that be? It's barely seven o'clock." He went to answer the door and soon came back, leading Elizabeth into the kitchen.

"Elizabeth!" Maria said. "What are you doing here?"

"I'm sorry it's so early," Elizabeth apologized. "But I really need to talk to you, Maria. Um, alone, if that's OK."

"OK. Hang on." Maria grabbed a blueberry muffin and a napkin and led Elizabeth to the family room, where they could talk undisturbed.

Elizabeth perched on the edge of the couch. "I don't know how to tell you this, but— First, let me ask you something. Did the thief take your video-tape, the one of the Boosters?"

Maria stared at her, her brown eyes wide. "Elizabeth, you came here at the crack of dawn to ask me about that stupid movie again?"

"It's important, Maria," Elizabeth pleaded. "Just tell me—did the thief get that videotape with all the others?"

Maria took a bite of muffin and chewed thoughtfully. Then she pushed her dark curly hair out of her face. "Actually, I guess he didn't. I was so disgusted with the movie that after I got home, I just threw it to the back of my closet. It's probably still there, under my dirty gym socks."

Elizabeth jumped up. "All right! Maria, we have to find it!"

But Maria sat where she was, eating her muffin. "Not until you tell me what this is all about."

Elizabeth abruptly sat down again. To Maria's surprise, she looked guilty. "I think the thief was after that videotape. That specific one," Elizabeth said.

Maria took a deep breath. "What do you mean? Are you saying he's a glutton for punishment?" Maria couldn't help smiling at her own joke. "Are you saying we were robbed by the Bad Video Police?"

Elizabeth smiled ruefully. "Not quite. Don't you see? You were filming *during* the robbery at Precious Stones. And the camera wasn't *only* on the Boosters. Because of your, uh, eclectic filming technique, you actually filmed practically the whole area around Precious Stones."

Maria stared at her in shock. "Oh, my gosh, Elizabeth, do you think maybe I filmed the crook without knowing it?"

"Yeah, maybe. When you told me only the videos had been taken, it didn't really hit me. But last night I started to put things together. There might be clues or suspicious characters on your tape, and that's why the thief took it."

"But Elizabeth," Maria asked, "how could the thief possibly know about my videotape? Even if he saw me filming that day, how did he know who I was and where to find me?"

Elizabeth hung her head and looked embarrassed. "I'm afraid that's my fault," she admitted in a small voice. "On Tuesday I went to the mall to see what I could find out about the third robbery. There was a cop there, and I asked him if I could see the police reports. He said no, but when I was talking to him I mentioned that we had been witnesses to the first robbery—and that you had been filming the Boosters. I gave him our names and addresses. I'm really sorry, Maria."

Maria frowned. "Do you think the cop is the thief?"

Elizabeth shook her head. "No. But other people were hanging around there, looking at the store. Someone might have overheard me. Then they panicked and decided to get the tape back at any cost. It's all my fault."

"But why would the thief be loitering at the scene of the crime? Wouldn't he try to get away as fast as possible?"

"You would think so, but actually, if the thief is who I think it is, it's part of his disguise that he *wouldn't* leave the mall after a robbery." Quickly, Elizabeth filled Maria in on Jessica's MacDuff theory.

"Wow. That makes sense. He *is* the one element connected to each of the robberies. Come on, let's find the tape right now!"

They ran upstairs to Maria's room and started digging through the clothes on the floor of her closet.

"Peeyew," Maria said, wrinkling her nose. "Sorry, Elizabeth. I really need to do a wash. But I found the tape!"

"Right under your dirty gym socks." Elizabeth laughed. "No wonder the thief didn't bother looking here."

Maria slapped her arm playfully. "It's almost time for school. Let's let the tape, uh, air out all day, and we'll watch it this afternoon."

"OK, but we should hide it carefully—in case the crook comes back," Elizabeth said seriously. "Let's ask Amy to come, too. Six eyes are better than four, when it comes to looking for clues."

"I can't believe my stupid tape might actually be useful after all," Maria said happily as they trooped downstairs.

Outside, they hid the videocassette in the fork of an oak tree in Maria's backyard.

"There," Maria said, climbing back down. "No one will find it now. It'll be a good place for it to get some fresh air, too."

"I can't wait till this afternoon," Elizabeth said. "I feel like we're finally on the right track!"

*   *   *

"No, no, Jessica. You're on the wrong track!" Ellen Riteman shouted. Ellen, a fellow Unicorn, had come to watch the latest event in the best-Booster contest on Thursday after school.

For this event, Winston had decided that Jessica and Lila had to ride their bikes over an obstacle course involving mud puddles, small bumps, and a low ramp. They had created the course in a corner of the local park.

Jessica skidded to a stop. "Where? Wasn't I supposed to turn left here?"

Tamara shook her head. "Nope. Back up and go through that puddle again."

Jessica did as she was told, thankful that Steven had helped her put new off-road tires on her bike just the day before. He had charged her five bucks, but she was sure it would be worth it. Jessica splashed through the puddle easily, went up and over a small speed bump, then made a sharp right turn on the narrow track. The ramp was coming up. In her practice run, she had wiped out here and fallen on her bike. But she couldn't do that now.

Come on, Jess, you can do it, she told herself. *You know you can do it. Just get up enough speed, then lift the handlebars the way Steven showed you.* Biting her lip in concentration, ignoring the muddy water trickling down her legs, Jessica raced toward the ramp at top speed. *Come on, now. Come on . . .* At the top of the ramp she jerked hard on her handlebars to lift the front end of her bike into the air. Then she was over the ramp and sailing toward the other side. With a jarring thump her back wheel landed heavily, then her front. Her teeth clamped with the impact, and for a second she felt the bike skid sideways under her. With adrenaline racing through her system, she righted herself, rolled another ten feet, then slowly braked. She had done it!

"All right!" she yelled. "Jessica Wakefield is through and clean! A perfect round! The crowd cheers!"

The small crowd of Unicorns and Boosters wasn't unanimous in its applause, but several of Jessica's closest friends did clap and cheer. Janet, Tamara, and a few others just looked stony-faced.

Lila rode up on her expensive metallic-purple European racer. She skidded to a halt and gave Jessica a withering glance. "You forget, Jessica, that if I go through clean, I'll still win the contest. I can't wait to be on top of the pyramid. And I can't wait to see what my fabulous costume will be." Lila pulled down her racing goggles and snapped the cuffs on her leather driving gloves.

"Go!" Ellen dropped the handkerchief tied to a stick that they were using as their flag. Lila sank onto her seat and started pedaling. It was clear from the start that her bike's thin, elegant tires weren't well suited to the off-road track. Twice she slipped a little as she rounded turns, and she almost wiped out on one of the low bumps. But score-wise, she was doing as well as Jessica as she headed toward the mud puddle.

Pedaling fast, Lila aimed her bike right into the middle of the puddle, clearly hoping that sheer momentum would take her through. But the mud was just too much for her narrow tires, and with a shocking jolt, her front wheel bogged down.

"Oh, no!" Lila's eyes were wide behind her goggles as the sudden stop practically threw her over the handlebars. Bouncing down hard into her seat again, she scrabbled for a grip, but the jerky motions made the whole bike start to topple over.

"Lila, watch out!" Janet yelled.

Finally, with a strangled yelp, Lila lost the balance battle and fell sideways with a loud plop—right into the puddle. She blinked in horror, sitting practically waist-deep in a sopping wet puddle of yucky, oozy mud.

"Lila," Jessica said sweetly, trying not to laugh, "you look so great in brown."

"You'll pay for this, Jessica," Lila snarled, whipping off her goggles. Her face was splattered with mud, but there were two white circles around her eyes. Even Janet couldn't stifle a giggle, and soon the whole crowd of Boosters was snickering behind their hands.

"I'm sorry, Lila," Grace said. "But you look like a raccoon."

"Oh, shut up," Lila said, getting to her feet with a loud sucking sound. "The course was rigged. But I'll see you guys at the tiebreaker tomorrow. Be there or be square." Still frowning angrily, Lila tugged her bike out of the mud and started rolling it home.

"Be where, Lila?" Jessica called.

"At the mall!" Lila tossed her muddy hair back over her shoulder. "Four o'clock!"

Nine

◇

"Elizabeth, this is so cool," Amy said. "I'm glad Sophia let me have an advance copy of your restaurant review. I can't wait to eat at the Dog House."

Amy, Maria, and Elizabeth were walking to Maria's house after school on Thursday. Elizabeth was impatient to watch Maria's movie again, but at the same time, she was glad Mrs. Slater would be home with them. If the thief had realized that he didn't have the right tape yet, who knew what would happen?

"Read it to me," Maria said, swinging her backpack.

"OK. Get this: 'The Dog House deserves an A for effort. Their imaginative presentations of everyone's favorite ballpark snack will be sure to win over the most sophisticated palate. This reporter sampled the Hot Chop Suey Dog, which features a turkey dog served on a bed of crispy fried noodles with a Chinese stir-fry side dish. One of my fellow reviewers raved over the Firehouse Dog, which was a traditional hot dog smothered with three-alarm chili. Another reviewer, whose appetite never ceases to amaze this reporter, was satisfied with the Sled Dog: two linked sausages served on two connected buns, with the diner's choice of any five toppings. I won't discuss the toppings, in order to spare those with weak stomachs.' Who was that—Todd?" Amy guessed, looking up.

"You got it. It's almost scary how much food he can vacuum up."

"Here we are," Maria announced, turning into her walkway. She unlocked her front door, and the three girls said hello to Mrs. Slater. Ten minutes later, the tape had been retrieved from the tree outside and they were settled in Maria's family room with a plate of cookies and three glasses of juice.

"OK, let her rip," Elizabeth said.

"This is going to be so painful," Maria moaned, popping the tape into the VCR.

"I'm all ready to take notes," Amy announced.

Just as when they had watched it before, the film opened with a large pink blob slowly backing away to become Maria's hand.

Maria groaned and covered her eyes. "I can't watch this again. It's totally mortifying."

"Maria, you have to," Elizabeth said firmly. "We all have to watch it for possible clues. I especially want to see if Mr. MacDuff appears anywhere in it."

So they sat and watched it—all ten minutes of it. They saw the left side of Elizabeth's face with hazy mall activity in the background, Elizabeth telling Maria to point the camera at the Boosters, the Boosters lining up, then Elizabeth's sneaker with her pinkie toe sticking out.

"That's a great shot of your toe, Elizabeth," Amy teased. "Maybe this video would convince your mom to buy you some new sneakers."

"Those are my most comfortable ones," Elizabeth protested.

More Booster shots passed by, then even Elizabeth couldn't help snickering at the shot of Janet's pimple.

On and on they watched, but although they looked carefully, they didn't see anything that seemed like a clue. When the movie was over, Maria sighed and clicked off the VCR.

"Whew, that was bad. Like getting a cavity filled," she said forlornly.

"We have to watch it again," Elizabeth said.

"What?" Maria cried. "No, Elizabeth. Don't make us!"

"Rewind it," Elizabeth directed.

They watched the entire thing again.

"One more time," Elizabeth insisted.

Both Maria and Amy groaned. "Elizabeth, my eyeballs are going numb," Amy complained.

They watched it again. Right at the section where the small, fuzzy, upside-down Jessica was getting ready to hurl herself at the already crumbling pyramid, Elizabeth grabbed the remote and switched the image to slow motion.

Very, very slowly, the small Jessica ran toward

the pyramid. The camera was focused mainly on a white column in the middle of the mall. Shadowy figures were floating slowly past the camera, the clown handing out balloons, a young mother with a baby carriage, the security guard . . .

"There he is," Elizabeth breathed. "At least we've placed Mr. MacDuff at the scene of the crime."

Then the VCR played the eerie, muffled sound of crashing glass, followed by a low, foghornlike alarm going off. Elizabeth leaned closer to the screen, holding her breath. The blue uniform of the security guard was barely visible behind the white column. The camera shook and jiggled and wobbled its way over to the broken glass. Then, as Elizabeth watched with all her concentration, she saw it: the clue she had been waiting for.

"Oh!" she gasped. "Did you see that?" She grabbed the remote and rewound the tape a few seconds. "Did you see what I saw?"

"I'm not sure," Maria said. "I think I saw something. . . ."

"It was a hand," Amy breathed. "Wasn't it?"

Elizabeth hit the "play" button, and the tape began to play in slow motion again. This time, all three girls saw it. At the very bottom of the screen, small and out of focus, a hand was pulling a gold watch out of the corner of Precious Stones' broken window.

"Wow!" Elizabeth jumped up and punched the air. "A clue! We found a clue!"

Maria and Amy jumped up, too, and they all high-fived each other.

"Now what?" Amy asked. "Whose hand was it?"

"That's what we have to find out," Elizabeth said grimly. "I think it was MacDuff's—we could see his uniform right behind that white column."

"Let's go to the mall and check him out," Amy suggested.

"Cool," Maria said, heading for the door. "I can't believe my video actually has a clue on it," she said happily. "Maybe I should be a photojournalist, after all. What do you guys think?"

"OK, now. We're looking for MacDuff," Elizabeth said at the entrance to the mall. "Just watch for any suspicious behavior. Like if he seems to be checking out a place. Or if he looks guilty. That kind of thing."

"Okey-dokey," Amy said.

"Should we split up?" Maria asked.

Elizabeth considered it. "Nah," she decided. "Let's just hang out and look like airhead middle-schoolers."

"You mean, look like Unicorns?" Amy said wickedly.

Elizabeth and Maria laughed.

"Exactly," Elizabeth agreed.

For the next forty minutes the three girls wandered around the Valley Mall, trying to look as though they were innocently window-shopping. Maria even went into Hot Minis and tried on a skirt that was on sale.

"I don't know if we have to look *this* realistic," Elizabeth muttered, glancing at her watch. They had circled the mall three times, and there was no sign of Mr. MacDuff. "Either he's not on duty, or he's hiding somewhere, planning the next robbery."

"My feet are tired," Amy complained. "How about if we stop for a snack? What places do you still have to review for the *Sixers*?"

"I guess we might as well sit for a minute," Elizabeth agreed. "I haven't been to Ding How's, Spuds 'n' Stuffin', Figaro's, or Chicken Lickin'."

"Let's try Spuds," Maria suggested.

"Fine with me," Amy said.

They found a table that looked right out onto the main strip of the mall. Elizabeth ordered curly fries, Maria tried bacon-cheese potato skins, and Amy got a small side order of mashed potatoes with gravy.

"Hmm, this looks good," Amy said, digging into her mashed potatoes.

"How's it taste?" Elizabeth asked, taking out her notepad.

Amy paused, savoring the mouthful of hot mashed potatoes. "Hmmm. I'd have to say it's a good mashed potato, but not a *great* mashed potato. It has a deep, mellow potato flavor, but the texture is almost a little too smooth. Not enough like homemade." She frowned and took another bite. "Strong gravy, but a little too much salt. Overtones of butter, and a satisfying, mealy potato aftertaste." She nodded decisively.

"OK, OK," Elizabeth said, writing quickly. "I think I got that. Maria?"

Maria was already halfway through her bacon-cheese potato skins. "Hang on," she mumbled. Then she swallowed and took a sip of her soda. "OK. I think my potato skins were more successful than Amy's mashed. These are the perfect potato skins: crispy on the outside, soft and crumbly on the inside. The bacon is real, not bacon bits, and the cheese is a strong, yummy cheddar. In short, these potato skins could serve as an example to every other potato-skin wannabe." She took another bite.

"Wow. Can I have a taste?" Amy asked.

"No. Get away." Maria said, laughing, but she gave her a small one.

Elizabeth sighed, looking out to the mall. "This is going to be a great review, but still, this trip is kind of a waste. I was hoping to be able to gather some more evidence."

"At least we've figured out that Mr. MacDuff could have made it from behind the white column over to Precious Stones' window as fast as he seemed to on the video," Maria reminded her.

"That's true." Elizabeth ate her last curly fry. "These fries were really good. Crispy, hot, and not too greasy. Just the right amount of salt and paprika. They don't even need ketchup. I think this place is going to get three and a half thumbs up."

Maria and Amy nodded their agreement.

"Hey, we better go," Maria said, glancing at her watch. "My mom is supposed to pick us up in about thirty seconds."

Just as the girls were leaving Spuds 'n' Stuffin', Elizabeth grabbed Amy's arm. "Look," she whipered. "It's Mr. MacDuff! Only, he's in regular clothes. Look what he's doing!"

"It looks like he's reading the menu of Ding How's," Amy said uncertainly.

"It *looks* that way, but I bet he's really casing the place!" Elizabeth whispered. "I wonder if that's going to be his next target. We have to stay and watch him."

"Elizabeth, we can't," Maria said. "I bet my mom's already waiting outside. We shouldn't be late."

For a moment, Elizabeth was torn. She watched Mr. MacDuff in front of the Chinese restaurant and wished that she could stake him out all night, for as long as it took. But she knew she couldn't keep Mrs. Slater waiting. And if she missed this ride, her parents wouldn't be too thrilled about having to come get her.

Finally she gave a deep sigh and turned to go. "Come on. We'll just have to let him go this time."

"You should have seen the creature from the mud lagoon," Jessica gloated that night after dinner. "Otherwise known as Lila Fowler." She cackled with glee. "It's funny, but I never noticed how well mud goes with the color purple. I wish I'd had my camera. I should have gotten Maria to videotape it. On second thought, it's a good thing I didn't. I mean, I would want to actually be able to watch it later." Still giggling, she flopped down on the family room couch.

Elizabeth couldn't help smiling at Jessica's good mood. "So the score is now three–three, right? What's the tiebreaker going to be?"

Jessica lay on her back and put her feet up against the wall behind the couch. "I don't know. We're going to meet at the mall at four o'clock tomorrow. Want to come and see your sister wipe the floor with Ferret Fowler?"

"Hmm—maybe. I have to review another restaurant, anyway. And I need to look at my map of the mall and study the exits. I decided to list all the stores that have been robbed, and then measure how far away the closest exit is."

Jessica rolled her eyes. "Elizabeth, you better not let Mom hear you talking about it. If she knew you were still on the case, she'd have a fit. By the way, how did my ingenious theory pan out?"

"I think you're right about MacDuff, Jess. But I need some solid evidence before I can do anything."

"Hm. Oh, well. What say we watch some tube?" Jessica picked up the remote and clicked the TV on.

At that moment, Steven came in. "I'll take that," he said, snatching the remote out of Jessica's hand. "It's time for *Highway Patrol*."

Jessica groaned. "Steven, that is the stupidest show. It's for total idiots. I don't know how you can watch it." She paused. "Oh. Never mind."

Steven turned to glare at Jessica.

Elizabeth giggled from where she was sitting in her father's easy chair. Nothing like a little sibling rivalry to take her mind off her own worries. As she watched *Highway Patrol* out of the corner of her eye, she wrote the first draft of her review of Spuds 'n' Stuffin'. Later she would type the final draft on her computer.

"This is a Channel Four Newsbreak," the TV announcer suddenly said.

Elizabeth looked up from where she was sitting.

Steven groaned. "Who cares? Get back to *Highway Patrol*," he groused, reaching for the remote.

"Wait, Steven—I want to see this," Elizabeth said, leaning forward in her chair.

Their local newscaster came onscreen, hastily adjusting his tie. "This just in. Yet another store at the Valley Mall has reported a robbery, in what is turning out to be Sweet Valley's worst crime wave in history. A new restaurant reported just minutes ago that its cash register was mysteriously emptied of all cash and receipts. Bill Mouzer is on the scene. Bill?"

"Ding How's," Elizabeth breathed. "It was the Chinese food place."

Steven looked at her. "What are you—"

His words were interrupted by Bill Mouzer appearing on the TV screen. "John, I'm standing here in front of Ding How's, the new Chinese restaurant at the Valley Mall. Just about an hour ago, an employee called 911 when she noticed that the cash register had been pried open. It's still unclear why the alarm system didn't go off. . . ."

In the Wakefield family room, Steven and Jessica turned to stare at Elizabeth, their eyes wide.

Ten

◇

Elizabeth looked at the clock hanging on the wall in her social studies classroom. *Please, please, ring. Come on, ring. You know you want to. Please ring.* Minutes away from the end of another school day, Elizabeth felt as though she would explode if she had to wait one more second to get out.

Glancing to her left, she caught Maria's eye. Maria gave her a sympathetic smile. Early this morning, Elizabeth had called both Amy and Maria and filled them in on the latest robbery. The girls had arranged to go to the mall after school to follow up on the MacDuff lead.

Despite her earlier misgivings, having her house broken into had convinced Maria that she had to get to the bottom of the mystery, dangerous or not. And Elizabeth's prediction about Ding How's had convinced Amy. After all, they had all seen MacDuff loitering in front of the restaurant. Elizabeth was glad that she had her friends' support. Even Christine Davenport, the heroine in Amanda Howard's mysteries, needed her friends sometimes.

Finally the bell rang, and Elizabeth grabbed her books and shot out the door. At her locker she threw some books in and took out others, scarcely noticing what she was doing.

"Elizabeth!" Jessica came up behind her. "I thought you were coming with me to the mall. You know, for the tiebreaker."

"Oh, sorry, Jess," Elizabeth said distractedly. "I mean, I'll be at the mall this afternoon, but I don't know if I can watch all of the tiebreaker. Amy and Maria and I are going to be tracking down that MacDuff character."

Jessica rolled her eyes. "Elizabeth, what is more important? Your very own twin sister being proved the best Booster once and for all, or some crummy little crime wave? I mean, where are your priorities?"

Elizabeth started to speak, but Jessica held up her hand. "Wait—don't bother to answer. I know you feel bad about it. Just try to stop by the contest at some point, OK?"

Elizabeth nodded, not trusting herself to speak. When Jessica had finally walked away, Elizabeth let out a small giggle.

Ten minutes later, when they walked through the mall doors, Elizabeth felt a tingle of anticipation.

"I really think something is going to happen today, guys," she told Maria and Amy. "We're on the right track, we're ready! Now, let's go, and keep your eyes peeled." She headed off toward the food court determinedly, her notebook and pen ready to jot down anything suspicious.

"Peeled eyes. What a disgusting image," Amy said, wrinkling her nose.

Maria nodded. "It's like that phrase 'keeping an eye on something.' Like you take out your eyeball and stick it on top of something to watch it. Yuck."

Elizabeth waited up for them. "Are you guys concentrating?" she demanded.

"Oh, yes," Amy and Maria said.

"Oh, no," Jessica said, her eyes round with horror.

"Yeah," Lila agreed. "Oh, no."

Janet Howell stood in front of the Dog House, her arms folded across her chest. "Why not?" she demanded. "It took us a long time to think of something that would be a good tiebreaker. What's wrong with a hot-dog-eating contest?"

"Janet, I'm still kind of queasy about the grapes. I just don't think this is a good idea," Jessica complained.

"I agree," Lila said. "Besides, we all know how much food Jessica can put away. It's not fair."

"Oh, really?" Jessica said, getting a dangerous look in her eyes. "Who's the only Unicorn ever to finish the Great White Whale sundae at Casey's? I thought ice cream was going to start coming out of your ears."

Lila's eyes narrowed. "Ice cream is different. It melts, and then it's smaller in your stomach."

"Bleah." Tamara made a face. "I don't want to think about what happens in your stomach, Lila."

"Look," Grace said. "We don't have time to think up another tiebreaker. Tomorrow's the big party. You two have to do this one. Now, let's go. Each of you choose your opening dog."

Glaring in resignation, Jessica and Lila read the billboard menu at the Dog House.

"I guess I'll start with the Dog Biscuit," Lila said grumpily to the server. It was a regular hot dog baked inside a large buttermilk biscuit, like a huge pig-in-a-blanket.

"Let me have the Dog-Eat-Dog," Jessica decided, choosing the small sausage stuffed inside a larger hot dog. "To begin with," she added fiercely to Lila.

Lila stuck her tongue out. The two girls sat opposite each other at a small pink table, their paper plates in front of them.

"Let the contest begin," Janet said.

"There he is," Elizabeth whispered, pulling Amy and Maria behind a large potted palm.

Across the wide main corridor of the mall, they could see Mr. MacDuff walking slowly away from them. He was swinging his nightstick and taking careful, measured steps. His head swiveled back and forth as he looked all around him.

"He seems like he's looking out for something," Maria observed. "Like for a burglar."

Elizabeth sighed. "Maria, don't be so naive. He's obviously casing the next place to rob."

"Oh. Are you sure?" Maria asked.

"Uh-huh. Watch him—where's he going? We have to follow him." Stealthily, Elizabeth crept out from behind the plant and ran to hide behind a thick white column. Amy and Maria followed her. As Mr. MacDuff walked farther away, the three girls ran from one hiding place to another, following him. At one point he waved hello to another security guard, and the two exchanged words that the girls couldn't hear.

"Do you think that other guy is part of the gang?" Amy whispered.

"I don't know," Elizabeth whispered back. "He could be innocent. MacDuff is the only one I'm sure about."

The girls tailed Mr. MacDuff down the mall corridor. They watched as he turned the corner to go down a service hall. Running silently over to the corner, Elizabeth poked her head around to look, just in time to see Mr. MacDuff disappear through a door.

She pulled back to consult with Amy and Maria. "He just went through a doorway," she said softly, excitement making her breathe hard.

"Was it a bathroom?" Maria asked.

Elizabeth shook her head. "No, I don't think so, but I'm going to find out."

"Elizabeth, you don't mean you actua—" Amy began. But before Amy or Maria could stop her, Elizabeth had crept quietly down the service hall. When she reached the door the guard had gone through, she looked up. It was marked "Private—Security."

Hah! Elizabeth thought. *Try, Private—Robbery!*

She looked back to see her two friends peeking around the corner, their eyes wide with trepidation. Maria waved for her to come back, but Elizabeth shook her head. Christine Davenport wouldn't back down now. Christine would follow the lead no matter where it took her—no matter what the cost.

Elizabeth tiptoed closer to the door. She took a deep breath. Very slowly and cautiously, she reached for the doorknob. She turned it. With one last look at her panicking friends, Elizabeth pushed the door open and slipped inside.

"How're you feeling, Jessica?" Winston asked. He dipped a paper towel in a glass of ice water and wiped her forehead. Then he massaged her shoulders and neck. "You're doing good, kid," he said. "Just loosen up, and easy does it. We have her cornered now—she's running scared. You're a champ, Jess. You're a contender. Just hang in there, baby.

"Come on!" Winston yelled, turning around. "What's keeping you? The girl doesn't have all day! Where's that dog?"

Grace ran over with a tray. "Sorry, Jessica. The line was kind of long. Now, which do you want? The Frankenweenie or the Poodle?"

Jessica hung her head into her hands. "What did I have last?" she asked. Her voice sounded thick and tired.

Winston checked his list. "You had the Puppy Pack. You know, the miniature hot dogs all bunched together?"

Across from her, Lila was taking a sip of diet Coke. "I don't think I'll ever eat another hot dog again as long as I live," she moaned.

Jessica fixed her with a withering look. "I don't think I'll ever eat *anything* again as long as I live." She looked up at Winston. "I'll take the Poodle," she said firmly.

Winston beamed. "Way to go, champ." He snapped his fingers at Grace. "One Poodle, please."

Grace hurried over and set a paper plate in front of Jessica. On it was a hot dog surrounded by french fries. Glaring at Lila, Jessica picked up a fry and grimly bit into it.

With a low snarl, Lila pulled her plate over and took a bite of hot dog rounds served with baked beans.

The crowd around them oohed and aahed in hushed whispers.

Out in the mall, Maria and Amy looked at each other.

"What should we do?" Maria asked softly. Her brown eyes looked worried.

"I don't know," Amy admitted. "I guess there's nothing to do but wait. I just wish I knew what was going on with Elizabeth, though. How will we know if she's in trouble?"

"I don't know," Maria said glumly. "This same thing happened with the charm-school mystery. Elizabeth kept things secret too long and ended up practically getting herself killed."

Amy sighed and sank slowly to the floor. "Well,

whatever she's doing, we just have to wait and hope that she's OK."

Maria sank down next to her. "Yeah," she said, checking her watch. "I hope she comes out soon."

Behind the door marked "private" was another hall, Elizabeth discovered. Silently she slunk down it, glad that her sneakers made no sound on the gray industrial carpeting. About twenty feet down the hall was another door, which was open. A square of light poured onto the carpet in front of Elizabeth, and she paused just before the doorway. Someone was speaking inside. She thought she recognized the grouchy tones of Mr. MacDuff.

"Yeah, that's what I said," he growled into the phone. "I tell you, I'm almost ready to quit this joint. As soon as I get another job taken care of, I'll be out of here."

Outside in the hall, Elizabeth gasped, then clapped her hand over her mouth. *Breathe slowly. Don't let him know you're here.* As silently as she could, she opened her notepad and began jotting down notes of what the man was saying. It sounded totally suspicious—as though MacDuff was planning another robbery right then and there!

"No, no, you worry too much. It's a piece of cake. No one suspects a thing. All I have to do is keep cool and quiet and everything will be OK. What? No, won't be long now. Maybe one, two days. Then we'll be sitting pretty."

Eyes wide, Elizabeth scribbled hastily in her notepad. This was incriminating evidence if she'd ever heard it! But how should she tell the police about it? How would they react to her listening to someone—well, basically, spying on someone— without a warrant? Did private detectives even need warrants? These were important details she would have to figure out. Now, if only MacDuff would give a few more details about which store he was going to hit next . . .

"No, of course not," MacDuff continued harshly. "That wasn't my fault. No one blames me."

They're gonna start blaming you when I get through with my report, Elizabeth thought, her face stern. She crouched by the door's opening, writing down as much as she could. MacDuff was obviously talking to one of his cohorts, a partner in crime. Elizabeth looked past the doorway down the hall. She needed to find another phone extension—she might be able to listen in on the conversation. She needed to know who MacDuff was talking to. Then she could blow this case wide—

"Oh!" she gasped as a rough arm hauled her off her feet.

Eleven

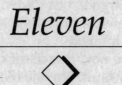

Sighing, Maria asked Amy, "How long has it been now?"

Amy looked at her watch again. "Two years, three lifetimes, and twelve minutes," she said. "Why isn't she back by now? What's going on? Why does she always put us through this?"

Maria shook her head. "I don't know. I'm starting to think I'm a bigger idiot than she is, because I'm sitting here getting involved in this whole thing."

Amy nodded. "I know what you mean."

"One more bite, Jess," Winston said encouragingly. "Come on, you can do it. Just one tiny, little, weensy more bitaroonie, just for me, OK?"

Jessica's head was dipping low over her plate. The large napkin that Winston had tied around her neck was spattered with grease and ketchup. Her movements, as she picked up her hot dog, were slow and jerky.

Across from her, Janet was wiping Lila's face with a cold, wet paper towel. The last few bites of a Firehouse Dog were sitting in front of her, slowly congealing on the paper plate.

"OK, so maybe a really spicy dog wasn't the way to go," Janet consoled her. "I mean, it made you drink a lot of Coke. But you're doing great, Lila. You have her whipped. Just a few more bites, and you'll be the best Booster forever."

"I can't," Lila said dully, her eyes glazing over.

"Lila," Janet coaxed, "just picture yourself on top of the Booster pyramid at every middle school game, from now on. Picture yourself leaping to the top as the crowd roars. . . ."

Lila lifted her head a fraction of an inch. The tiniest spark of life entered her eyes. Across from her, Jessica was trying to lay her head down on the table, but Winston was pulling her back up.

"Lila, imagine yourself on top of the pyramid, waving to the crowd," Janet whispered into Lila's ear. "You're waving, flashbulbs are popping, the crowd cheers. Everyone's looking at you, you're giving a big Booster smile . . . Not only that, but you'll get to choose the coolest costume tomorrow. What if it's really fabulous? What if it makes you look like a model, and a talent agent spots you? You never know—it could happen."

Taking a deep breath, Lila sat up in her chair. Almost mechanically she reached for her Firehouse Dog. She took a bite and chewed. Behind her, the crowd of Unicorns, Boosters, and innocent by-standers broke into spontaneous applause.

Jessica lifted her head off the table a fraction of an inch and blearily gazed at Lila. Then, with a thunk, her head dropped back down.

"Jessica, come on!" Winston cried. "This is the final round. You're on the mat, but you're not out yet! Come on, Jess, we're depending on you." He stood up and practically began tearing out his hair from the tension.

"I'm gonna barf," Jessica mumbled against the table.

Terrified, Elizabeth looked into the angry eyes of Mr. MacDuff. She had been concentrating so hard on writing her notes that she hadn't realized he had hung up the phone and was walking toward the door.

"What are you doing here, kid?" he said angrily, still gripping her arm painfully.

"N-nothing," Elizabeth stammered. *I should have had a story ready in case I was caught*, she realized in dismay. *Christine would have.* "Uh—I was looking for the ladies' rest room," she said quickly.

Mr. MacDuff grimaced with suspicion. "Oh, really? Well, maybe you can't read, kid. That door was marked 'private.' I guess you thought it would be fun to break in here, huh? Were you trying to steal something?"

Elizabeth gasped. He had some nerve, to accuse *her* of stealing when *he* was the one who everyone knew was behind the mall robberies! "Of course not!" she snapped. "You *would* suspect that right off, wouldn't you?"

Mr. MacDuff frowned, and his eyes narrowed. "Look, kid, I don't know what you're talking about, but I know someone who might." He plunked Elizabeth firmly into a metal chair in front of his desk and reached for the phone.

Elizabeth tried not to show any fear. Who was he calling? His accomplices? An underworld thug? Was an unmarked van going to pull up to the delivery entrance and take her away without Maria and Amy knowing? Elizabeth swallowed hard.

Mr. MacDuff thunked the phone down in front of her and picked up the receiver. "Call your parents," he ordered.

For a moment Elizabeth felt an overwhelming rush of relief. In the next second she realized what the phone call would mean, and her stomach knotted up. With Mr. MacDuff's eyes glaring into hers, she slowly took the receiver and started to dial home.

Tight-lipped, Mrs. Wakefield held Elizabeth's arm and marched her across the mall. Mr. Wakefield strode behind her, carrying Jessica in his arms. Her hand was across her eyes, and she was moaning faintly.

As Elizabeth walked quickly, trying to keep up with her mother's angry pace, she glanced over and saw Maria and Amy hiding behind a small palm tree. She managed to wink once, and shrug almost imperceptibly. Maria nodded, pressed her index finger to her lips, and slunk farther back behind the plant.

Even though she knew she was in major trouble, Elizabeth couldn't help feeling proud of Amy and Maria. They had kept their cool, even when they hadn't known where she was or what had happened to her. Now, standing behind the palm, they were almost invisible. Out of the corner of her eye, Elizabeth saw Amy make telephoning motions with her hands. Elizabeth nodded, getting the message. Amy would call her later. She just hoped she would be allowed to take the call.

Her mother bustled her out of the mall and across the parking lot to the Wakefields' van. Mercifully, Steven hadn't come with his parents to witness the final humiliation of both twins. Elizabeth was in total disgrace. Her parents were so angry, they hadn't even decided on a punishment yet. They had simply muttered words like "grounded," "punished," "allowance," and "forever." Elizabeth sighed.

Mr. Wakefield laid the almost unconscious Jessica across the backseat as though he were loading a sack of potatoes. Jessica whimpered slightly and tried to curl up into a fetal position, her eyes shut.

Elizabeth was forced to sit between her parents in the front seat for the brief, silent ride home.

"So basically, Joe, the situation is I have one sister who's too smart for her own good, and one sister who's too dumb to get a clue," Steven said into the phone. He took a bite out of his apple and crunched loudly into the receiver. He was talking to Joe Howell, who was his best friend and Janet's older brother.

"I know. Can you believe it? I can't decide who's more of a blockhead." Steven laughed. "Oh, man, why didn't Janet tell you? I would have given a lot to be there." He laughed again. At that point Jessica wandered into the kitchen like a zombie, her face pale and her blue-green eyes listless. "Oops, I gotta go, Joe. Duty calls." He hung up the phone and took another bite of his apple.

"Hey, Jess, how's it going? I was wondering if I could do something for you. You know, like if you need me to put a bucket by the side of your bed or something." He chewed cheerfully.

Jessica didn't bother to reply. She just shuffled out of the kitchen listlessly. Steven heard her dragging herself upstairs again.

Mr. Wakefield came into the kitchen from the family room. "Steven," he said sternly, "we don't need you to make things worse. Just chill out, OK?"

"Sure, Dad," Steven said sulkily. *Geez. My dopey sisters set themselves up for some perfect teasing, and I can't even take advantage of it. It's just not fair.*

Up in her room, Elizabeth sat on her bed glumly. She was grounded for two weeks. No mall, no friends' houses, no after-school activities. And no detecting ever again. She sighed. Her notepad full of all her clues was on the floor, and she tapped it with her foot. A fat lot of good it would do now.

And the most frustrating thing was that for all her effort, for all her thinking and planning and detecting, she still had only rumors and hearsay—no hard facts. She sighed again and flopped back on her bed. Some detective she was.

"Lila, honey, just take another sip of this Alka-Seltzer," her father pleaded.

Lila was propped up on a fat pillow on the leather couch in the Fowlers' family room. Although she wanted to die, there was a part of her that was enjoying her father's doting attention. He was so rarely at home, and so busy when he was, that to have him hovering over her now, all worried and concerned, was very satisfying.

Lila raised her head a little. "I can't, Daddy. It's awful."

"But it'll make you feel better, sweetheart, I promise." Mr. Fowler held the fizzing glass out toward her. He plumped the pillow in back of her so that she could sit up more.

Lila begrudgingly took a tiny sip, then grimaced. "Bleah."

"I know," Mr. Fowler said soothingly, brushing her hair back away from her face. "Poor thing. Why don't you just nap for a while, and I'll wake you up when it's time for your favorite TV show. OK?"

"OK," Lila said in a pathetic voice. She felt fat and bloated, and a little nauseous, but otherwise not too bad. Tomorrow she would definitely feel better. Just in time to choose the coolest costume for the big, invitation-only black-tie party at the mall.

Later that night, as Elizabeth was getting ready for bed, her mother came in and sat down next to her.

"Elizabeth, do you understand that we don't want you snooping around like this for your own good?" Mrs. Wakefield said. "Every time I remember the danger you put yourself into with the charm-school crooks, I panic all over again. I just can't have you risking your safety—and possibly the safety of others—just to satisfy your curiosity."

"I understand," Elizabeth said stiffly. "But Mom, you should have heard Mr. MacDuff talking on the phone. He was saying totally incriminating stuff. I just know—"

"Elizabeth Wakefield, you know no such thing—not definitely, anyway. I want this matter dropped, as of now. Is that clear?"

"Yes," Elizabeth said in a small voice. Her mother kissed her goodnight, and Elizabeth turned off the light and settled down against her pillow. *I bet Christine Davenport's parents never ground her for investigating.* Sighing sadly, Elizabeth thumped her pillow with her fist and tried to go to sleep.

She was in the Valley Mall. Elizabeth looked around, but she felt as though she were swimming, wading slowly through weirdly thick air. No one else was around—the mall was empty. Elizabeth started walking.

As she went down the main mall corridor, she noticed that the stores had been rearranged. Right in front her was Precious Stones. It wasn't called Precious Stones anymore. Instead of a store logo above the door, it had a huge, fluorescent number one. Elizabeth walked on.

The next store was Hello Again, although in real life it was actually at the other end of the mall. It had a big number two where its sign should be. After that came the electronics store where Todd had bought his earphones. It had a brightly lit number three above its entrance.

Soon she came across Ding How's, which for some reason had been moved right into the middle of the walkway, blocking Elizabeth's path. It was called number four, and the numeral was picked out in sort of Oriental-looking type.

Her hands on her hips, Elizabeth looked at Ding How's, then back at stores one, two, and three. *There's a clue here,* she thought. *I just have to find it.* Suddenly she heard a commotion in back of her, and she spun around.

It was Mr. MacDuff, and he was running right toward her, his nightstick raised. Elizabeth gasped and pressed herself into a dark corner of Ding How's, praying that he wouldn't see her. But he continued to run right at her, yelling something and waving his nightstick angrily.

Shrinking down as small as she could, Elizabeth covered her eyes with her hands. Mr. MacDuff's thundering footsteps echoed on the mall's tiled floor. Elizabeth braced herself for the blows. But his heavy footsteps passed her by. When she looked up in disbelief, she saw that he had really been chasing a huge chicken, who was running down the mall, squawking furiously and flapping its wings. As Elizabeth watched, Mr. MacDuff chased the chicken first into store number one, then number two, then number three, and finally right past her into store number four. The chicken was squawking and screaming. When they had pushed through the swinging doors into the restaurant's kitchen, Elizabeth darted out from her hiding place and ran away.

Soon she found herself running down a long, dark hallway. It was the service hall that she had gone down earlier. She was thinking, *I shouldn't do this. Mom and Dad will kill me,* but she didn't seem able to stop. Finally she paused in front of the door marked "Private—Security," and she hesitated only a moment before shooting through the door. Inside, she sped down the narrow hallway and darted into the room where Mr. MacDuff had taken her before.

There was a man there, wearing a clown suit. In one hand he held a bunch of silver helium balloons. Elizabeth stood openmouthed, staring at him. Then he reached down with his other hand and opened a pink bag marked "Clues."

"Here you go, little girl," he said in a pleasant voice. "One clue per customer." He began to pull out the clue, and Elizabeth leaned forward anxiously. His hand came out a tiny bit at a time, farther, and farther . . .

"Elizabeth, Elizabeth, wake up. Come on."

Elizabeth grumbled and rolled over. She couldn't wake up now—she was about to get a very important clue. Sleepily, she waved away whoever was bothering her.

"Elizabeth, please—it's an emergency." An insistent hand shook her shoulder.

Groaning, Elizabeth turned to face the annoying voice. There was no way she could go back to sleep now. And just when she was about to receive the most important clue of the case!

"What?" she snapped. "What is it?" She opened one eye to see Jessica standing anxiously in front of her.

"I need to borrow your hot-pink socks," Jessica said urgently. "I'm having a total wardrobe crisis." She sat on the edge of Elizabeth's bed and bounced up and down a few times.

Sighing, Elizabeth looked at the ceiling. Then she looked over at Jessica. "How do you feel today?" she asked.

Jessica shrugged her shoulders. "Well, I've stopped feeling like I'm going to slip into a coma. But I still don't feel like eating anything. I can't stand even to smell food. And if I never see another hmm-hmm again, it'll be too soon."

"Another hmm-hmm?" Elizabeth asked.

"Yeah, you know—it comes on a bun. Just don't say the words in front of me, OK? Anyway, I'm convinced Lila cheated on that tiebreaker somehow, but what's done is done. I'll let her have her little day in the sun for now, but I'm already plotting to reclaim my position on top of the famous Wakefield pyramid. So can I borrow your hot-pink socks? They always cheer me up."

Elizabeth waved toward her chest of drawers. "Go on, take them."

Twelve

◇

"Kimberly, are those shoes new? They're adorable," Grace Oliver said. It was Saturday evening, and the Boosters had gathered at Jessica's house to get ready for the black-tie party. Each Booster had to wear black tights, black shoes, and a black turtleneck, so that the costumes would stand out.

Jessica finished french-braiding her hair in front of the mirror. "I wonder what our costumes will be like," she said, tying a black ribbon at the end of her braid.

"Well, I don't really have to worry," Lila said smugly, leaning toward Jessica's mirror to put on some mascara. "Since I get first pick, I know that I'll end up looking cool no matter what. You, Jessica, on the other hand, might not be so lucky." Lila smirked. "I mean, I hope you don't end up in a Minnie Mouse costume or anything."

"Well, Mrs. Richter said that we'll each represent

a food-court restaurant. So our costumes will probably be international somehow," Tamara explained.

"I can't wait," Winston said. He was lying on Jessica's bed, tossing a baseball up in the air and catching it. He was wearing black jeans, black sneakers, and a black turtleneck. "Maybe I'll get to be a samurai."

Grace came to sit next to him. "How come you don't have to wear tights?" she teased him. "No fair."

Winston grinned. "As the only male Booster, I get special privileges. Besides, I don't have the legs for it."

"Elizabeth, could you get the door?" Mrs. Wakefield called.

Elizabeth was already on her way. Although she was grounded, her parents were allowing her to have Amy and Maria over for the evening.

"Hi, Elizabeth," Amy said when Elizabeth opened the door.

"Hi, Elizabeth," Maria said loudly. "I brought the tape, like you asked," she added in a whisper. "But I don't understand why you want to see it again."

Elizabeth put her finger to her lips and said, "Shh. I'll tell you after my parents leave."

Just then Mrs. Wakefield appeared at the top of the stairs. "Hi, Amy. Hi, Maria."

"Hi, Mrs. Wakefield," they chorused.

"You look really nice, Mom," Elizabeth said.

The Wakefields had been invited to the black-tie

party at the mall because Mrs. Wakefield had been a design consultant for the project. Mr. Wakefield was wearing a tuxedo, and Mrs. Wakefield had on a long, midnight-blue evening dress.

"Thank you, sweetie," Elizabeth's mother said. "Steven's going to stay home with you tonight, but you can call the mall information number if you need to get in touch with us, OK?"

"OK," Elizabeth said.

"And remember, you can't go anywhere with Amy and Maria."

Elizabeth hung her head. "OK, Mom." She turned to Maria and Amy. "Let's go see how Jessica's doing."

The door to Jessica's room sprang open and she popped out. "How do I look?" she asked, doing a little twirl.

"Very New Yorky," Maria said, looking at Jessica's all-black ensemble.

Jessica looked down at herself. "We're supposed to wear all black, for our costumes. Actually, I was relieved that I could still get into any of my clothes."

Amy nodded. "After yesterday," she said.

"Yeah. Anyway, I guess we're about ready to go." She leaned back into her room. "Come on, Boosters!" she yelled. Boosters started trailing out of her room and down the stairs. Jessica turned back to Elizabeth. "I wish you could come, Elizabeth."

Elizabeth nodded. "I know, but even if I weren't

grounded, I still wouldn't be able to go to the party. It's invitation only, and no kids allowed."

"At least Steven will stay home and keep you company," Janet simpered as she walked by.

Rolling her eyes, Elizabeth said, "Yeah, lucky me. Well, have a good time, you guys. I hope your costumes are terrific."

Jessica hugged Elizabeth. "Listen, how bad could they be?" she said philosophically. "If worse comes to worst, I'll end up being a geisha or something. See you later." She ran down the stairs, where her parents were waiting to give all the Boosters a ride to the party.

Elizabeth stood at the top of the stairs and waved good-bye to everyone. As soon as the last Unicorn was gone and the front door slammed behind them, Elizabeth turned to her friends.

"All right!" she cried. "Let's go watch the tape again!" She started to pound downstairs toward the family room.

Amy groaned. "Elizabeth, do we *really* have to watch it again? I mean, no offense, Maria, but I feel like if I watch it one more time, I'm going to run screaming down the street."

Maria grinned. "I feel the same way."

Elizabeth turned around at the bottom of the stairs. "Come on! I had an amazing dream last night, about the mall robberies. I know there's an important clue that I'm missing. It's right in front of my face, I can feel it. I have to see the tape again."

Sighing, Maria started to walk downstairs. "OK,

OK, one horrible home movie, coming up."

"Hello, children," Steven said as they stopped in the kitchen to get some soda.

"Hey, Steven," Amy said breezily. "Eating again? How unusual."

Elizabeth giggled as she got out three glasses.

Steven frowned and put down the cold leg of chicken he was munching on. "Listen, Amy, I'm in charge while my parents are gone. You better watch it, or I'll bounce your butt out of here."

Amy rolled her eyes. "Oh, stop, stop, I'm trembling in fear. Make him cut it out, Elizabeth," she said in a bored monotone.

Steven picked up his glass of soda and drained it in one long gulp. Then he thumped his chest with his fist and let out a huge, quavering belch.

Maria watched, fascinated. "Brothers are so interesting, Elizabeth. More interesting than sisters. Does he do laundry?"

"Not often," Elizabeth admitted.

In the family room they put the tape in the VCR and sat down to watch it again.

"So in this dream," Elizabeth said, "a clown was reaching into a bag marked 'Clues.' I got the feeling it was important."

"OK," Amy said. "Let's look at that hand again in the movie."

They fast-forwarded to the spot where the fuzzy, out-of-focus hand was reaching into the broken window at Precious Stones. As soon as the hand came onscreen, Elizabeth paused the tape so that the image was frozen. Then she crawled on her hands and knees over to the TV set and practically pressed her face against the glass.

"What is that shadow?" she murmured. "Guys, do you see this line going across the hand? What is it?"

Amy and Maria came over to peer at the fuzzy image on the TV. Maria squinted, backed away, and squinted again. "I don't know," she said. "It just looks like a shadow to me. Like a shadow fell across the hand as it was reaching out."

"Wait—back it up a second," Amy said.

Elizabeth flicked the remote, and the image rewound a little bit. The girls watched, and again in a corner a fuzzy white hand slowly withdrew a gold watch from the broken window.

Amy suddenly sat up straight. "It's a scar," she said excitedly.

"What?" Elizabeth cried.

"It's a scar." Amy paused the tape and pointed to the screen. "This hand has a scar on it. Definitely." Her finger traced along the shadowy line.

"I think you're right," Maria said. "Wow." Her eyes glittered with excitement. "Elizabeth, this is what your dream meant. It meant that the hand itself was a clue! Now all we have to do is find someone whose hand has a scar."

"Omigod!" Elizabeth gasped. "I know who it is!"

Thirteen

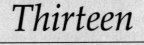

"OK, girls," said Mrs. Richter, the woman who was in charge of the food-court promotions. "And boy," she added, smiling at Winston. "I have your costumes here. As I mentioned, each costume will represent one of the new food-court restaurants. Remember, when you're in your costume, you're not only representing that restaurant, but also the Valley Mall, and even Sweet Valley itself. So I expect you to behave like little ladies and gentlemen tonight." She beamed at the group of Boosters, who were eyeing her warily.

The Boosters had gathered in the mall management office as soon as Mr. and Mrs. Wakefield had dropped them off. Now Mrs. Richter was explaining their duties.

"Once you're in your costumes, you'll each be given a tray of hors d'oeuvres to pass around to our guests. I'd appreciate it if you waited until all the guests have been served before you actually eat anything yourselves. Now, are there any questions?"

Lila raised her hand. "May we see the costumes now?"

"Certainly," Mrs. Richter said. She bustled into another office and came back with a bundle of plastic dry-cleaner bags full of colorful costumes. "OK, who's first?" she asked.

"I am," said Lila, shooting Jessica a triumphant look.

Jessica ignored her. *So what if she gets first pick and I get last? So I'll end up being a Mexican dancer or something. That's cool.*

Lila rustled through the bags. "Oh, this one is pretty," she said, pulling it out.

"That's for Ding How's," said Mrs. Richter. "It's a traditional Chinese silk dress. It's called a cheongsam."

Great, Jessica thought. *That's fabulous. I'm home free.* The dress was made of sky-blue embroidered silk and was long and closely fitted, with a slit up one thigh. Jessica knew Lila would look totally glamorous in it.

"Great," Lila said, and went into the bathroom to change.

"I'm next," Janet said bossily, pushing her way to the front. She pawed through the bags and chose a cute farm girl outfit for Spuds 'n' Stuffin'. It had a pair of short denim overalls, a red-checked blouse, and a blond wig with two braids.

No prob, Jessica thought.

Winston chose the costume for Taco Shack, which was a white shirt, a colorful Mexican serape, and a sombrero. He put it on with a grin and pretended to do a stomping Mexican hat dance.

For Figaro's Pizza, Grace ended up with a white toga trimmed in gold, and leather sandals that laced halfway up her legs. A plastic olive branch perched on her dark hair. "Toga party!" she cried, spinning in a circle.

A gaudy fruit-print Hawaiian shirt, sunglasses, and a straw sun hat was Tamara's Smootharama costume.

Come on, come on, Jessica thought. *Let's get it over with.*

"What do you mean, you know who it is?" Maria asked Elizabeth.

Elizabeth stood up and excitedly began pacing the Wakefield family room. "Well, that's what my dream was trying to tell me. It ended up being about a hand. Now we see in the video that the robber's hand has a scar on it. And"—Elizabeth spun around to face her friends—"I've seen that scar myself, in person!"

Amy gasped. "You have? When? Where? Was it MacDuff?"

Frowning, Elizabeth sank into her father's easy chair. "I don't remember exactly, but it has to be," she said. "Think about it. It's the hand of some stranger, that I've seen up close recently. How many people's hands have I seen? But when MacDuff caught me in the hall, he sat me down in his office and handed me the phone. That must have been when I saw his scar—when he gave me the phone!" She wiggled in her chair. "I'm telling you, this is the proof we need!"

"But what are we going to do about it?" Amy asked.

Elizabeth thought for a moment. Then her eyes grew round. "Do you guys think he's going to be working tonight, at the party?"

Maria nodded. "It would make sense. I'm sure the mall would want all the security they could get."

Elizabeth's face turned serious. "You know what that must mean. He's planning another robbery for tonight!"

"Then we have to stop him!" Maria cried.

Finally, there were only Jessica and Kimberly left waiting for costumes. Jessica didn't feel too nervous. It was Lila's being on top of the Wakefield pyramid that was going to be the problem.

Kimberly smirked at Jessica and looked through the last two bags. She frowned and glanced up at all her friends, admiring one another's cute outfits. Then she looked through the bags again. Jessica saw her clench her teeth.

Kimberly grabbed one bag and flounced angrily into the bathroom to change. Hesitantly, Jessica picked up the last remaining bag and pulled the costume out of it. As she held it up in front of her, her eyes widened with horror and shock.

Oh, no, it can't be. It can't be. There must be some mistake.

One by one, the other Boosters noticed her standing there, her costume clutched in her hands. Lila giggled, and Grace covered her mouth and turned away. Kimberly came out of the bathroom, and even though she herself was dressed as a large, fluffy white chicken, she still managed to laugh at Jessica.

"OK, put this on," Elizabeth ordered, handing Maria a fancy blouse with a lace collar.

The three girls were in Elizabeth's room, changing into party clothes.

"Do you really think we'll blend in at the party?" Amy asked doubtfully, pulling on some black velvet leggings.

"Well, no," Elizabeth admitted, brushing her long blond hair. "But I'm hoping to at least get in. Then I'm going to try to get my parents to help." She grimaced. "I hope they won't be too mad. But I know we're doing the right thing."

"That makes one of us," Maria muttered, putting on some lip gloss.

"Let's bring the tape with us and your video camera, Maria."

Maria groaned. "I was afraid you'd say that."

Elizabeth grinned with anticipation. "I just hope we get there before he strikes again!"

Ten minutes later the girls got off the bus in front of the Valley Mall. Inside the double glass doors, they stopped and stared in amazement. The mall interior had been transformed. Decorations were everywhere—paper flowers, streamers, balloons, hundreds of twinkling white lights. It looked like a fairy tale.

"Wow," Maria breathed as they walked forward to stand in the entrance line waiting to get into the food-court atrium. "The mall will never be the same."

"It's beautiful," Amy agreed.

As far as Elizabeth could see, they were the only kids in line. Dressed-up people were passing through a little entranceway up ahead, where they could check their coats and present their invitations.

"Invitation! Oh, no," Elizabeth exclaimed. "I forgot." She thought quickly, then turned to Maria and Amy. "If anyone asks, we're covering the event for the *Sixers*, OK?"

They nodded their agreement. Looking ahead, Elizabeth could see a young, fair-haired guy taking people's coats and handing them tokens. She frowned, trying to place his face. Then it came to her.

"Look at that coat-check guy," Elizabeth whispered to her friends with a giggle. "Just last week he was working at Sound Trek. Then he was working at Chicken Lickin'. Now he's doing this. Poor guy. I guess he just can't hold on to a job."

Amy nodded. "You know, that guy was our waiter last night at Ding How's." She grinned. "He must have worked the most jobs in mall history!"

Elizabeth smiled. Obviously the guy needed some kind of career counseling. He'd never get ahead if he couldn't stay in one place. At last it was their turn to pass through the entranceway. Elizabeth shrugged off her mother's fancy evening wrap.

"Reporters for *The Sweet Valley Sixers*," she said briskly, holding out her wrap. She casually looked around at the party. "Here to cover the event."

"Certainly, miss," the coat-check guy said with a smile. He reached out to take her wrap.

As though in a dream, Elizabeth saw his long,

pale hand reaching toward her. The same hand that had given Todd his new headphones. The hand with a long, pink scar on it.

The robber's hand!

Numbly, Elizabeth took the token he handed her, remembered to smile thanks at him, then turned away in a haze. She slowly drifted over toward a bank of potted plants.

"Elizabeth, look!" Maria cried. "A huge chicken! Just like in your dream. What do you think that means?"

Kimberly Haver passed them, an angry scowl on her face. She was in a fluffy white chicken suit and was carrying a large tray of barbecued buffalo wings from Chicken Lickin'.

Maria turned to grin at Elizabeth, then noticed the weird expression on her face. "Elizabeth, what's wrong? Are you feeling all right?"

"That guy," Elizabeth whispered hoarsely. "The coat-check guy."

"What about him?" Amy asked.

"He's the robber!" Elizabeth said. "I saw the scar on his hand."

Amy and Maria both gasped. "Are you sure?"

Elizabeth nodded quickly. "I definitely saw it. It must have been that guy all along. After all, he's worked at both Sound Trek and Ding How's. And he must have been the clown handing out balloons in back of us when you were filming the Boosters, Maria. In my dream last night, when Mr. MacDuff was chasing a chicken, it was because the last job I knew that guy had was at Chicken Lickin'. I just can't believe I was so wrong about Mr. MacDuff. All the clues pointed in his direction." She shook her head.

"What do we do now?" Amy asked.

Just then Lila ambled by, carrying a tray of mini-eggrolls and steamed dumplings from Ding How's. "Hey, kids," she said in a syrupy voice. "Hors d'oeuvres?" She held the tray out to them.

Lila smirked. "Have you seen your sister yet?" she asked Elizabeth.

"No, why?"

Lila smirked again. "You'll understand when you see her. Gotta go—gotta mingle." She moved off again into the crowd.

"Omigosh!" Elizabeth said, clapping her hand over her mouth. "Maria! I just realized that that guy must have been the one who ransacked your house! He's dangerous! I think we should tell security about it right away," she said, looking around. "And see if you can inconspicuously videotape him when he isn't looking. Use the zoom lens to focus in close on his hand."

"OK," Maria nodded. "I can do that."

Amy pointed through the crowd. "There's Mr. MacDuff."

Elizabeth groaned. "Oh, no. I'm sure he hates me. But I guess he's the only security person we've got." She headed off toward him, Amy and Maria following her.

"Mr. MacDuff?" Elizabeth asked hesitantly.

He looked down at her. "Yes? Oh, it's you." He frowned.

"I have something to tell you," Elizabeth began.

*   *   *

"You look very nice, honey," Mrs. Wakefield said to Jessica. "Very professional."

"I don't want to talk about it," Jessica said woodenly. "Hors d'oeuvre?" She held out a tray toward her parents.

"Mmm, little pigs-in-a-blanket," Mr. Wakefield said, popping one in his mouth. "My favorite." He chewed happily for a moment, then he frowned.

"Alice, isn't that Elizabeth over there?"

Mrs. Wakefield and Jessica both looked. Then Mrs. Wakefield frowned, too. "It *is* Elizabeth. What is she doing here? She's supposed to be grounded."

Jessica shrugged wearily as her parents moved off to confront Elizabeth. She walked through the crowd, taking tiny steps, which were all her costume permitted. "Hors d'oeuvre?"

Mr. Fowler took a pig-in-a-blanket and munched it. Then he looked down and cocked one eyebrow. "Good heavens, is that you, Jessica?"

"Yes, Mr. Fowler," Jessica said sadly. "I know I don't look like myself."

"Nonsense, my dear, you look very—cute."

"Uh-huh," Jessica said. She gave him a tiny smile and moved off into the crowd again. "Hors d'oeuvre, anyone?"

"Kid, listen," Mr. MacDuff said, scratching his head. "I got enough on my plate right now without you—"

"Elizabeth! And Amy and Maria," Mrs. Wakefield said sternly. "What are you doing here? I thought I made it clear that—"

"Mom, Dad, you have to listen," Elizabeth pleaded. "I'm telling you, we have the evidence on videotape. Just let me explain."

"Yo, Jessica," Bruce Patman said, coming up to grab a pig-in-a-blanket off her tray.

"Hello, Bruce," Jessica said coolly. "Don't bother to tease me about my costume. I've heard it all already."

Stuffing the hors d'oeuvre into his mouth, Bruce looked Jessica up and down. He smiled meanly. "What costume?" he asked.

Jessica's eyes narrowed as Bruce turned away. *That does it. I've had it. The Boosters can stuff this costume. I've got to get out of here,* she thought. *I don't have to take this abuse.*

"Elizabeth," Amy whispered, tugging on her sleeve. "That guy is looking at us."

Elizabeth turned around and looked over at the coat-check guy. Sure enough, he was staring right at her, her parents, and Mr. MacDuff. His eyes looked pale and suspicious.

"Maria," Elizabeth said softly, "try to get him on tape."

Maria casually pulled her video camera out of her large shoulder bag and backed behind a column. Then she held the camera up to her eye and pointed it at the guy. Elizabeth stepped over and tapped her on the shoulder. "Lens cap," she said softly.

Maria swung the camera down and popped off the lens cap. "I knew that," she said.

Mr. MacDuff was speaking on his walkie-talkie.

"George, I need you to verify someone's security clearance, please. Yeah. It's the young guy working coat-check. Uh-huh."

Elizabeth stood with her parents, Amy, Mr. Mac-Duff, and Maria and waited nervously. All the grown-ups were skeptical, but she couldn't really blame them. She hadn't bothered to mention the little fact that she had arrived this evening convinced Mr. MacDuff had been the burglar. Why complicate the issue?

"Elizabeth, he's still watching us," Amy whispered, turning around quickly to glance at the coat-check guy.

The guy was looking more nervous all the time, and he was openly staring at Mr. MacDuff now. He was standing by the party entranceway, and to Elizabeth he looked like a cat about to take off, all tense and wiry.

Please hurry, George, whoever you are, Elizabeth thought anxiously, watching Mr. MacDuff talk. *He's going to get away.*

Suddenly, right in front of Elizabeth's eyes, the guy took on a panicked expression. Elizabeth looked around and saw that Maria had slowly edged out from behind the column. She and her camera were clearly visible now.

"Mr. MacDuff!" Elizabeth cried, but it was too late. By the time the security guard had lowered his walkie-talkie, the guy had already turned around, jumped over a table, and started to run.

Fourteen

◇

"Catch that guy!" Elizabeth screamed, pushing her way through the crowd to follow him. Without thinking, she broke into a run. Grown-ups in evening dresses and tuxes turned to stare at her as she rushed past, trying desperately to keep an eye on the mall robber.

With Amy, Maria, and Mr. MacDuff running close behind her, Elizabeth shot through the entranceway to the party and headed out into the mall. She could hear her parents calling for her to stop, but she couldn't. Not now.

"There! Up ahead!" she yelled, pointing at a barely visible light-blond head running through the mall. The suspect was weaving in and out of the crowd, narrowly missing people, almost toppling a display of greeting cards. He turned to look back once, and Elizabeth saw the panic in his eyes.

There was a sound of rustling, then a crash behind her. "Oof!" Amy grunted.

Elizabeth looked back just in time to see Amy wipe out in a bank of potted plants. But Elizabeth couldn't stop to help her—she kept running.

In front of her the coat-check guy darted down a hall, then almost as quickly popped back out again and ran even faster down the main mall corridor.

Must have been a dead end, Elizabeth thought. She was panting now, and her throat hurt. If only she could run faster . . . Two teenage girls up ahead froze when they saw the guy running right at them. They look as if they couldn't make up their minds which way to jump. Elizabeth grimaced when she saw the robber plow right through them, as if he were a full-back. The girls screamed and clutched each other, but they lost their balance and one of them toppled into the center fountain with a big splash.

But the guy kept running.

Mr. MacDuff's pounding footsteps on the mall's tiled floor sounded louder and louder, and Elizabeth realized he was catching up with her. They had gone almost the entire way around the mall.

Finally, MacDuff pulled up alongside Elizabeth. "Kid, stay back," he huffed. "Guy . . . might be dangerous . . . might . . . have a gun . . ."

"I have to get him!" Elizabeth panted. "I solved the mystery!" Her lungs were burning now, and her feet hurt. All she wanted to do was lie down on the floor and take a lot of slow, deep breaths. But she couldn't. Not while the Valley Mall burglar was still on the loose.

*   *   *

I'll just sit down for a minute, Jessica thought sadly. She plopped down on a little bench not too far from the food court. It was pretty well hidden by a large cornstalk plant. She swung her feet over the edge, back and forth, thinking about her troubles. *This whole thing has been a disaster,* she admitted to herself. *I look like a total fool in front of everyone. There's no way I can salvage my reputation.* She sighed again and rested her chin in her hand. A few wisps of her long blond hair drifted into her eyes and she brushed them back, tucking them beneath her costume.

Vaguely, she became aware of the sounds of a commotion coming closer to her. It was probably some stupid parade for the food court, she figured. Still, it almost sounded like people running and shouting. Wearily, she got to her feet, a little unsteady in her heavy, stiff costume. She shuffled to the edge of the cornstalk plant and poked her head out. Her eyes widened. About twenty feet away, Mr. MacDuff was chasing Elizabeth! They were both yelling, and Elizabeth was waving her arms. Mr. MacDuff was trying to stop Elizabeth from exposing him as the mall burglar!

Making a snap decision, Jessica jumped out from behind the plant. "Stop!" she shouted, then POW!

Something hit her at full force, throwing her body back several feet. She landed hard, and her head smacked against the floor. Then everything went black.

Oh, no, Elizabeth thought. The mall robber was headed right for the main mall exit. Once he was outside, she knew they would lose him in the huge parking lot. She didn't know whether Maria had managed to get a close-up shot of his hand with her video camera, but even if she had, how would the police ever find him again?

Right behind a big cornstalk plant, the main entrance loomed. If only something would stop him somehow.

Then, right before Elizabeth's eyes, a huge, human-size hot dog jumped out from behind the plant.

"Stop!" the hot dog shouted with Jessica's voice.

Then everything seemed to happen in slow motion.

The thief wasn't able to stop, and he ran full tilt into the large, tan hot dog, knocking it over heavily. He was thrown totally off balance and sprawled through the air as though shot from a slingshot. After flying several feet, he smashed headfirst into the solid cement planter. He hit with a sickening thump and slid unconscious to the ground.

Elizabeth skidded to a stop just in time. A glance told her Mr. MacDuff was running over to the robber and handcuffing him to a little bench. Elizabeth ran to the hot dog, who was lying on the ground, her thin black legs and feet sticking out from her bun.

She rolled the hot dog over and saw Jessica's face, groggy and confused.

"Elizabeth," Jessica said. "I didn't want MacDuff to get you."

Kneeling on the floor, Elizabeth pulled Jessica's

head onto her lap. "You're a hero, Jessica," she said, almost crying with happiness. "You stopped the mall robber. You're a hero."

Jessica smiled dazedly. "No, Elizabeth. I'm not a hero. I'm a hot dog."

Fifteen

"Let me see! I want to see it!" Jessica tried to grab the newspaper away from Elizabeth, but her twin held it away.

"Hang on, Jess. We can look together."

It was Sunday morning, and Elizabeth couldn't wait to see what the *Sweet Valley Tribune* had to say about the mall robber.

Next to her, Jessica squealed with delight. "There's a picture!" She looked at it more closely and frowned. "Oh, no. There's a picture."

Steven hovered over them, then let out a gleeful snort. "That's a good shot of you, Jess. It captures the real you. And your mustard stripe looks nice and fresh."

Mr. and Mrs. Wakefield came into the kitchen, still in their bathrobes. Mrs. Wakefield smiled. "How are my two heroes this morning?" she asked. She examined the bruise on Jessica's head, then kissed it.

"Fine, Mom," Jessica said.

"Listen to this," Elizabeth said. "'Elizabeth Wakefield, working with security guard Leonard MacDuff, was in hot pursuit of the alleged mall robber. With impressive teamwork, her twin sister, Jessica, leapt out with perfect timing and stopped the thief cold. The two girls are to be commended for their bravery. The robber, Percival Henderson, was caught with detailed plans of the security systems for several stores at the mall. It's anyone's guess where this heartless thief planned to strike next. But we can all sleep well tonight, thanks to the Wakefield twins.'"

"We're very proud of you both," Mr. Wakefield said. "Although Elizabeth did totally disobey our orders by going to the mall last night."

"And by getting involved in this mystery at all, which we expressly told you not to do," added Mrs. Wakefield.

"And by dragging Amy and Maria into it, which their parents are pretty unhappy about," Mr. Wakefield continued.

Elizabeth hung her head, her excitement about solving the mystery deflated.

"Am I still grounded?" she asked.

Her parents looked at each other. "Well," said her father, "we've decided that you can't go to the mall for a week. But you can see your friends and participate in after-school activities."

Elizabeth smiled. "To tell you the truth, I don't think I'll really feel like going to the mall for a while."

Her parents laughed, and Mr. Wakefield started making a pot of coffee.

"That's it?" Steven demanded. "Just because she happened to solve a little mystery almost by accident, she gets off the hook?" He looked outraged.

"That's enough, Steven," Mrs. Wakefield said in a warning tone.

"Yeah. That's enough, Steven," Jessica mimicked, sticking her tongue out.

"Kids, do we have to eat out again without you?" Mr. Wakefield asked in exasperation.

"No!" all three of them shouted.

"So apparently Mr. MacDuff was talking to his wife that day on the phone when I overheard him," Elizabeth told Maria and Amy as they walked toward Maria's house. It was after school on Monday, and they were going to Maria's to watch the video she had taken at the mall party Saturday night, just for fun.

"He was just explaining that he was going to line up another part-time job, and then he'd have enough money so that he could quit the security job. His wife was worried about his safety, especially with all the robberies."

"After the robber was taken to the police station, Mr. MacDuff actually seemed much nicer. I guess all the robberies were making him grumpy," Amy said.

"Yeah, I almost feel guilty for ever suspecting him," Elizabeth admitted. "I was following the wrong trail the whole time. Christine wouldn't have made the mistakes I did," she said thoughtfully. "I really need to brush up on my detecting skills. Maybe with a lot more practice . . ."

"Elizabeth!" Maria and Amy groaned together.

"Well, maybe not for a while," Elizabeth conceded.

They walked up to Maria's house, and a few minutes later they were settled in her family room with cookies and glasses of orange juice.

"OK, let's roll 'em," Elizabeth said, pointing the remote.

At first there was blackness, then Elizabeth's voice said, "Lens cap."

The blackness exploded into a riot of color as the camera swung down to the ground, and Maria's voice said, "I knew that."

Then the camera swung up again and panned crazily around the party. It lingered on the dessert table, where platters were heaped with pastries, candy, and cookies.

"Nice shot," Amy murmured.

"Too bad you didn't get any of Jessica in her hot-dog costume," Elizabeth said with a smile. "She actually looked kind of cute."

Maria sat forward as the camera jerkily moved sideways until it focused on the robber's face. He seemed to be looking right into the lens with his almost colorless eyes, and the three girls shivered.

"What a creep," Elizabeth said softly.

"Yeah," Maria agreed solemnly.

The camera lurched downward, slipped past his hand for a second, then stayed fixedly a bit to the right. None of the robber or his scar was showing at all. Fuzzy, elegant people milled around in the background. Then a large, shiny red object loomed onscreen, taking up almost half of the TV image.

"What the heck is that?" Amy wondered.

Maria looked at it hard. She tilted her head first to one side, then to the next, trying to make it out.

At last it came to her. "That, for your information, is someone's big, sequined butt!" Glaring at the TV, Maria snatched the remote away from Elizabeth and clicked the image off.

Shrieking with laughter, Elizabeth and Amy rolled on the floor.

"Tell me, Ms. Film Director," Amy said, laughing, "what were you trying to say with your use of red sequins?"

"Very funny," Maria snapped. "You're just so funny." She stood in front of the TV with her arms crossed. "I'm throwing that stupid camera away. It's obviously just broken. There's nothing I can do with it."

Amy and Elizabeth just laughed harder.

"It's nice to be friends again," Lila said, taking a sip of her Oreo milk shake. She was sitting across from Jessica at Casey's after school on Monday.

"Yeah," Jessica agreed. She licked the ice cream off her straw. "Maybe we could even take turns being on top the pyramid."

Lila wiped her mouth with her napkin. "Don't hold your breath."

Jessica shrugged. She would deal with that problem later. Right now she was just glad not to be fighting with Lila anymore. In their own way, they were best friends, and Jessica had missed her.

The bell over the door at Casey's jangled, and Jessica looked up.

"Whoa," she said softly. "Who is *that*?"

The boy who had just come in stood at the counter, trying to decide what to get. He had dark-blond hair and warm brown eyes. Jessica had never seen him before. He was wearing a sweatshirt that said *Sweet Valley High*.

"I don't know," Lila said, eyeing the boy. "But he is definitely cute."

Jessica's blue-green eyes lit up. "We have to find out who he is. Maybe Steven knows him."

Who's the mysterious new boy in Sweet Valley? Find out in Sweet Valley Twins #82, **Steven's Enemy.**

SIGN UP FOR THE SWEET VALLEY HIGH® FAN CLUB!

Hey, girls! Get all the gossip on Sweet Valley High's® most popular teenagers when you join our fantastic Fan Club! As a member, you'll get all of this really cool stuff:

- Membership Card with your own personal Fan Club ID number
- A Sweet Valley High® Secret Treasure Box
- Sweet Valley High® Stationery
- Official Fan Club Pencil (for secret note writing!)
- Three Bookmarks
- A "Members Only" Door Hanger
- Two Skeins of J. & P. Coats® Embroidery Floss with flower barrette instruction leaflet
- Two editions of *The Oracle* newsletter
- Plus exclusive Sweet Valley High® product offers, special savings, contests, and much more!

Be the first to find out what Jessica & Elizabeth Wakefield are up to by joining the Sweet Valley High® Fan Club for the one-year membership fee of only $6.25 each for U.S. residents, $8.25 for Canadian residents (U.S. currency). Includes shipping & handling.

Send a check or money order (do not send cash) made payable to "Sweet Valley High® Fan Club" along with this form to:

SWEET VALLEY HIGH® FAN CLUB, BOX 3919-B, SCHAUMBURG, IL 60168-3919

NAME_____

(Please print clearly)

ADDRESS_____

CITY_____ STATE_____ ZIP_____

(Required)

AGE_____ BIRTHDAY_____ /_____ /_____